A Ruined Wife

The seductions,
submissions, and
sexual encounters
of ordinary housewives

Andrea's Story
Part II

Seduced Tramp

by Mrs. Jennifer Nite

FOR ADULTS ONLY

About This Edition

This is a revised edition of the wildly popular eBook available on Kindle. You may ask if the revisions are worth purchasing the paperback. Good question.

The front and back cover photos have changed. (Yes, boys, the lady is a married friend of mine). There are also many grammatical fixes. Finally, there are substantive changes throughout the book which provide more detail in certain areas of the story. Parts II and III in particular have much more detail. The chapters have also been revised, for a total of 40 chapters through the end of Part III. All told, the three parts total well over 500 pages.

That all being said, I usually use eBooks on my iPhone just to pass tedious down time, such as when I'm trapped in an airport waiting hours for a flight. Personally, I am the kind of person who has to own a copy of a book if it's in print. There is just nothing like holding a hard copy of a book in your hands. It also makes it easier for your spouse to innocently "find" the story lying around the house!

– Jennifer

Introduction

The ordinary.

That's the life of most people. We get up in the morning, we go through the work day waiting for it to end, and we come home to take care of our children and husbands. And then we go to bed, roll over, and ... it starts all over again. Day after day. Year after year. The drudgery of married life. I know . . . I've experienced it myself for 16 years.

But sex is not ordinary. Sex is extraordinary. But inevitably sex leaves the marriage after a period of years. And what do you do then? Suffer through life?

This is a series that explores that question from the perspective of several married women, with loving husbands and often with young children. Some are younger ladies, and some are older.

The results are the same -- a sexual awakening that changes their lives. They become ruined to the ordinary sexually-empty drudgery of the monogamous marriage. And their husbands become accepting and often participating cuckolds (archaically known as wittols).

Is it a moral issue? I can't answer that question. It used to be that sexual awareness was a topic explored by men, and often (but not always) shunned by women.

The men's stag films and the pulp fiction novels of the 50s and 60s changed dramatically with the advent of the Internet. Morals widened, sexual freedom has expanded, and pornography is secretly available to everyone virtually for free. And women are now active consumers. MILF is now a universally known word. Being seen as a beautiful MILF is remarkably the goal of many wives and mothers throughout the United States and, indeed, the world.

The transformation of our society is what led to these stories. I do not pass judgment on these ladies or their husbands. I understand what a little on the side can do for one's outlook on life.

The stories speak almost exclusively of the sexual encounters of ordinary housewives and mothers, women I would consider to be genuine ladies. These are the women who are your next-door neighbor, the gorgeous wife you see at the PTO meeting, that tremendously hot girl you see at the office every day.

The places in these stories are everywhere, from their homes to their offices and everywhere in between.

Be warned! The tales of these married women are not for the lighthearted. Unlike most books in this genre, these books are not romance novels and they are not stories of lovemaking.

They are likewise not a collection of short stories that you have to read 10 pages to get to what you want, just to find that it's little or nothing. These are hard core, very explicit stories that get right to the point in great detail. They are XXX, no question about it. The wives present in graphic detail and usually from their perspective the circumstances that led to their seduction . . . blow by blow, so to speak.

It's mainstream encounters, from the single seduction -- often forced for the first time – to threesomes and even the occasional gang action. Their partners are white, black, and everyone else. But there are no water sports, no bondage, no whips and chains, no beating of people, no animals, no children, no incest, and no weird sexual acts. If you need any of that sort of thing, then you will need to go elsewhere.

You should also avoid these books if you are easily offended by filthy, sordid talk, because that is the essence of the seductions. So be careful! These books are so hot you'll burn yourself.

A word of warning before you continue. We won't patronize you, because we trust that you are all mature, consenting adults. But we caution you to seriously consider the ramifications before embarking on the lifestyle presented in this series. Provocative Publishers believes in the importance and value of family relationships.

Jealously and insecurity are the scourge of families. If you are considering an open-marriage kind of lifestyle, please do everything possible to preserve your family. You have a choice. Some people, like we will see with Andrea, didn't have a choice. The exhilaration of the lifestyle was forced upon her, after which she couldn't turn back!

So, if you want to hear the details of the seductions of beautiful housewives and the endless sex they have come to need -- how each has become ruined to the ordinary drudgery of married life -- then read on. You will not be disappointed with these tales of infidelity!

We invite you to read the whole series. They each tell a different story from a different perspective!

Who knows. Maybe some film producer would like to adapt these stories to the screen. There certainly aren't any good XXX films out there that present these kinds of stories versus all of that mindless stupid porn in the world. If you're an interested adult film producer, please give us a shout.

That all being said, let's continue with the second of my friend Andrea's story.

Where We Left Off

I have a long story to tell, so long that I've had to put it into three parts! I hope you've already read *Reluctant Tramp*, because it tells you how I was first ruined. My story gets more exciting!

To remind you of who I am. My name is Andrea, and I'm a horny housewife and mother! I'm now 36 years old, and I'm a pretty brunette wench. I continue to keep my body in shape, and my tits are as perky as ever.

My husband's name is Mark. We've been married for 11 years. Mark had been the only man I'd ever been with until I was broken in last year by an older stud named Bill.

My husband and I have had another baby girl since my last story, giving us two children. My other daughter, Ginger, is 9. And yes! I know it's Mark's because I haven't fucked another man since that day over a year ago with Bill and the black boys.

But things changed after I had that baby. I couldn't deny my inherent promiscuity. Mark wasn't satisfying me in bed. As much as I love him, he just wasn't. Our sex life remained dull, the frequency of the sex being sporadic at best. I guess my hormones were hornier than his!

I was sick and tired of using a dildo to take care of myself, constantly daydreaming about strange men taking me and using my body for their whorish needs. Just before I returned to work, I started using two dildos to DP myself, but it just wasn't enough.

My horniness started to become increasingly overwhelming. Thoughts of sex preoccupied my mind day after day. I was lascivious, plain and simple. Each day I fought the horny urges, trying to control the uncontrollable. As hard as I tried to be good, it was a bad situation that was bound to get worse.

It did.

This my continuing story of how some bastards ruined me -- or maybe saved me from a dull marriage with this new lifestyle. And now to the next part of my story . . .

Chapter 15

I took maternity leave at the end of my pregnancy, and then I went back to work about three months after I had a C-Section delivery.

It was hard to go back to work. I hated my job, I hated my sex life, I was sexually frustrated as hell, and I was miserable! My hormones were always in overdrive.

To make matters worse, strange men would come into the bank in every day and compliment me on my appearance. I had to say it felt great, especially after I had the baby.

Eventually I found myself looking over every man who came in, wondering how big his cock was. Each day I fought the horny urges, trying to control the uncontrollable.

There was little I could do. I was losing control. As hard as I tried to be good, it was a bad situation that was about to get worse. The urges were overwhelming. I kept thinking over and over, I had to get my cunt stuffed full of cock. Big cock!

I was so miserable, and it just made my marriage worse. I knew I couldn't deny myself much longer. But I didn't know what to do.

I returned to work to find that I had the same asshole boss. And this jerk was a true asshole. His name was Jack, an Asian man. I think his parents were boat people back in the 70s. He was about 5' 6", somewhat of a short man.

Jack always gave me a hard time. He jumped me whenever I was late, he constantly criticized my work, and he spoke condescendingly to me and the other women employees. How this asshole became a bank manager, I'll never know.

About a month or so after I returned to work, Jack called me into his office. I knew he was calling me in to chastize me. He had done it weekly since I got back, and it was getting old.

I walked in and he told me to shut the door. He then proceeded to yell at me yet again, this time for some trivial mistake that I hadn't even made.

"Goddamn, Andrea, can't you get anything right?" he said, "I've just about had it with you."

I couldn't take his bullshit any more. He was driving me crazy with all of his bullshit. I snapped back that it wasn't me who made the mistake, which infuriated him more.

Jack threw a pencil at me, which pissed me off. His homely, overweight features provided the perfect come back.

"You bastard, you must be a pencil-dick asshole who can't even satisfy your wife!"

"Fuck you, Andrea," he shot back.

His insults continued.

"You're no fucking dream date yourself," he snarled, "You should get on your knees and be thanking me for your job!"

Something snapped inside of me. That was it, and the gauntlet was down.

I marched up to the son-of-a-bitch, intent on showing him who the better catch was. He wanted me on my knees? No problem!

I looked in Jack's eyes, and the bastard gave me a cold look back. I dropped to my knees in front of him, determined to give this filthy bastard of the best blowjobs of his miserable life.

I swiftly unzipped his suit trousers and reached inside his pants before he could say a word.

"Ah, Andrea . . . ," he started to mumble.

"What are you . . ."

His words stopped as I pulled out his limp cock. I quickly stuffed the growing prick into my mouth. I reached around Jack and grabbed his ass, pulling his groin into my face. I started to suck with all of my being.

The cock tasted great, even though it was attached to an asshole. It brought back memories of the wonderful cock I had experienced that fateful day last year.

The cock inflamed me in no time. It immediately brought back all of the whorish emotions I had fought so hard.

"Andrea, you goddamned fucking slut!" he snarled, "What the fuck!"

He didn't complain for long. I pulled the cock out looked up at him with a whorish look in my eyes.

"Do you want me to stop?" I asked.

He was very curt.

"Not until you suck me off," he said.

Ready to show him my talents, I started to jerk the stiffening prick, popping the cock head into my mouth periodically and sucking on it.

The Asian prick rose to about 6" in all, very thin, not much of a cock I thought. Yep, he was a pencil-dick!

I took the throbbing fuck stick and snapped my lips around the cock head. I quickly jammed forced it into my throat.

"Ohhhh fuck," he said, loving my hot mouth.

"I never knew you were a little cocksucker," he mumbled.

I moaned to affirm his statement, and his words made me suck harder. I was intent on drawing cum from the bastard.

It was only a matter of minutes before Jack was ready to unload. I pushed my head backwards so I could look into Jack's eyes as he pumped his huge, thick gobs of hot scum into my throat. He really got off dumping his load.

I pulled the fucker out while he was still shooting, and a huge thick string of cum shot into my mouth. As I pulled the cock head out, cum ran from the leaking head and drooled down my lips.

My tongue darted out to catch it, and I ran the cum back along his still hard shaft. It must have been a sight for him to see me licking his cum up and down his stiff prick!

I licked the cum off from my lips and his shaft, giving a sluttish moan as I savored the sweet mixture of lipstick and cum. God, how I love that taste! I never forgot it from the episode last year.

I looked up at Jack, and I opened my mouth to show him the wonderful wad of cum he put there.

I swirled it around my lips and I got up and stood before Jack, my mouth still open and exposing his load. I closed my mouth and swallowed, making sure my neck showed him the proof.

I thought I would be his equal now, having answered his challenge so expertly. I was wrong. I only opened myself up to allow him to abuse me in ways the bastard never dreamed he could.

As I licked the last of his cum off from my lips with a slow, sultry wave of my tongue, Jack remarked very coldly.

"Get the fuck out of here, you fucking slut."

I went to my office and thought about the way I had snapped. When faced with the situation, I snapped into the role of whore and sucked off the son-of-a-bitch who tormented me at work. I wasn't even giving my husband any, but I went to such great lengths to let this bastard enjoy me.

And I was so wrong. How could I have been so wrong about how he would react? I couldn't believe the situation I put myself in.

I was still thinking about it when he called me back to his office that afternoon. I really thought that I was about to be fired.

Chapter 16

When I walked into his office, I was surprised when Jack gave me an order in a cold voice.

"Shut the door and lock it," he said.

I quickly knew what did the bastard wanted, and I was somewhat scared. His reaction was so unpredicted last time.

Jack walked up to me and gave me a icy look. He grabbed my arms and brought me to the front of his desk. Without saying a word, Jack pushed me over the desk with his hand, and quickly lifted my long dress. Seeing my silken white slip before him, he rubbed my ass and squeezed my cheeks.

Jack reached underneath my slip and felt the thin panties. He noticed that I had stockings on instead of pantyhose, which caused him to speak for the first time since he had me lock the door.

"I fucking thought so," he said, as he began to roughly feel up my hairy cunt.

Jack worked his hand through my slit, an action that was making me incredibly hot. I never realized before that the fucker was so hot for my ass. You sure couldn't tell from the way he treated me.

As he cupped and rubbed my cunt, it became readily apparent to me that Jack had dreamed of laying me for a long time. Maybe that is why he was such an asshole, because he couldn't have me.

Jack started to speak to me with filthy words, not knowing how it would set me ablaze.

"Andrea, you slut, you need a hard cock right here, don't you?"

Oh God! Here we go, I though! I gave Jack a sluttish moan in response.

The bastard wasted no time, as I could hear his zipper come down. He hiked up my dress and slip again, pushed aside my panties, and grabbed his hard shaft. Jack was ready for a piece of married ass.

The bastard guided the tip of his throbbing cock head and placed it at the entrance of my moistening slit. My cunt had been molded for large cock by Bill and Al, so I wondered how I'd feel for Lil' Jack. I knew Mark still loved my cunt, but he was at least somewhat large! But needle dick Jack?

Jack easily pushed the blood-engorged cock into me, my cunt readily opening to take it. My cunt snapped back pretty good from the baby that I could feel Jack's pencil dick.

Yep, needle dick. I could tell.

Small or not, I loved it. The feeling of that hot little dick caused me to groan in pleasure, and I again felt like a whore in heat as he pushed it into me.

Jack then grabbed me by the waist with his two hands, letting the top of my dress fall and rest on his prick.

"Andrea, you worthless fucking cunt, take my hard cock."

I had flashbacks of Bill and Al.

I moaned again when I heard the words, and he rammed the throbbing fuck stick all the way into me in one rough stroke. The feeling of my cunt being opened so rapidly caused me to grasp the other side of the desk and gasp.

It had been a year since the big-dicked studs took me last year. My cunt must have gone back to normal proportions, because it was apparently nice and tight for Jack. He didn't seem to notice that I was in reality a size queen.

"Ahhhhhh . . . fuck," he said, as my cunt snapped tight around his invading cock.

Before he only said bad things to me. Now he could fuck me while he said them, I thought. God! What depths I had fallen to!

Jack got more condescending.

"How does that bone feel, you fucking skank!"

I was pissed despite my lust. This asshole had no appreciate for what he had with me.

"I've had bigger," I blurted out.

My comment enraged the asshole. He start to brutally deep fuck me, forcefully slamming his balls against my ass with each hard stroke.

I didn't care. It only helped.

My cunt burned the feel of the fiery hot cock that was so ruthlessly hammered into it. It burned for a deep fucking, as it felt like such a long time since Al and his friends had enjoyed it. At least Mr. Pencil has a somewhat decent length cock. Yes sir, I was excited as hell and felt unusually horny when Jack began to bone my cunt.

"You fucking slut," he slurred.

"Fucking bitch!" he screamed, "feel my hard cock in your hot little cunt."

Unfortunately, as Bill and Al had conditioned me, I responded positively to the vile statements. I gave another whorish moan and started to thrash my head.

"I'll make you moan, you lousy cunt . . . you fucking tramp," he said, words I knew this man really meant.

With that, Jack started to screw me with a vengeance. The feel of Jack's fiery little cock felt great. He was no great cocksman like Bill or Al, but his cock was hard and filled my needs at the moment.

I pushed myself up and braced myself on the desk with my hands. I started thrusting my ass back to meet his horny thrust. Here I was, actively fucking the nasty bastard.

Jack continued to use my cunt to meet his own needs, grinding his cock in and out of me to the rhythm of his sordid statements.

"Take my cock, you fucking whore . . . take it."

"You goddamn horny little slut!"

I was getting in the mood with the nasty talk.

"Yes! Yes! Fuck me, please fuck me harder you bastard!" I begged back.

My needs were not his, however.

"Fuck you, cunt," he said as he thrust into me, blasting his spunk deep inside me with series of animal-like grunts.

Jack balled my cunt for only a few minutes before losing it. He failed to make me cum, and he didn't care in the least. I tossed it up to bad luck, thinking that my hot cunt brought too much pleasure to the man too quickly. But it did reaffirm that he truly was an asshole like I had always thought of him.

When Jack was done, he quickly stuffed his softening cock back into his pants, allowing my dress to fall down. I remained draped over his desk as I heard his pants zip up, his cum dripping down my legs. I was lost in lust, wishing there was more cock to satisfy my needs.

Jack quickly broke my whorish swoon with more degradation.

"Get out of here, you fucking tramp," he said as he grabbed my arm and briskly led me to the door.

"I'll let you know when I want to hump you again!" he said as he pushed me out.

Again, I went back to my office, feeling like a worthless tramp. I couldn't believe what I had done. I let that son-of-a-bitch Jack screw my husband's pussy, not to satisfy me, but only to empty his balls. I was nothing but a tight cum bucket for him. And I helped him by pushing back!

I sat at my desk bewildered at myself. Here I was with Jack's cum leaking out of me and dripping onto the chair. I resolved at that point to stop this degenerate situation.

If I could.

Chapter 17

Work was a new place for me when I went back the next day. I had sucked off my asshole boss and then spread for him, and the situation between us had now changed. Oh, did it change.

I had hoped my blowjob would cause him to be nice to me, to appreciate me. I was wrong. Jack used me as a cum rag yesterday afternoon, and I was afraid what this new day would bring. I knew I had to take charge of the situation and stop it before it got completely out of hand.

I saw my chance when Jack called me into his office about 10:00 a.m. If he brought up the day before, I thought, I would simply tell him that things got out of hand and that it would never happen again.

I was in for a big surprise. I quickly learned that Jack was not so ready to give up his sexy new sex toy.

As soon as I walked in, I shut the door. Jack looked at me devilishly from behind his desk.

"Lock the door . . . Time for my blowjob, sweetheart," he said.

I went and sat in a chair in front of his desk. I tried to explain to him that it was all an accident, and that I was a happily married woman. The bastard wasn't taking it. Jack stood up and marched over to the door, locking it.

I stood up, ready to leave.

Jack came over to me and stood before me. His stature and clear determination caused my resistance to quickly abandon me. He looked into my eyes with a stern expression and spoke very curtly to me.

"Fuck your husband," Jack said. "You started this Andrea, and it isn't so easy to just end it."

Jack then placed his two hands on my shoulders and pulled my head down towards his crotch.

"I want my blowjob," he said coldly.

A bulge was standing before me. My mouth was watering. I had to suck it. All resistance fled, my noble goal shattered.

I slipped off of the chair and fell to my knees.

"That's it," he said as he rubbed my hair.

"Unzip my pants and blow me!"

I reached out and unzipped the fucker's pants. As I reached in for his prick, he unbuckled his belt and let his pants fall to the floor. I quickly yanked his underwear down, too. Jack's stiffening prick bobbed in front of my face.

"Ah, give me head," he said.

Something in me caused me to submit my mouth to the bastard without a thought. I just had to taste that cock!

Jack's cock had a unique upward bend to it that I loved, curving up to my face. Grabbing hold of his throbbing cock, I looked up at him.

I was taken aback by the stern look on Jack's face. I stroked the cock a little to get it fully hard, and then slipped it into my mouth. I started to bob my head up and down on the needy fuck stick.

I must admit, the cock tasted great and I was somewhat relieved that I would at least get to taste another load of cum. I sucked Jack's shaft into my mouth, and then withdrew to bob my head faster and faster

As I got more aroused, I sucked the fucker's pole into my throat until my nose was buried in his musty pubic hair, the cock head firmly lodged in my gullet.

I pulled the fuck stick back out, and quickly thrust it back in. The next time there was a thick string of drool hanging from my lip and running to the cock head.

Jack loved it.

"Ahhhh . . . suck that cock dry, you horny bitch!" he said.

I ran my tongue over the head and along the bottom of the stiff hot cock down to his balls, every so often slipping it deep into my throat. I licked and sucked intermittently, enjoying my treat. Unlike yesterday, I also jacked his pole and reached up to rub his balls with my long fingernails.

Jack's eyes were fixed on me the whole time I administered to his needy cock. As he reached down to stroke my hair, a lusty groan escaped from him. He pulled my mouth onto his blood engorged cock, ready to use it like a cunt.

"Ohhhhh . . . you fucking cunt . . . you are a great cocksucking bitch!" he moaned.

Hmmm ... I finally got a compliment from the bastard, I thought.

I let out an uncontrollable sluttish moan when Jack complimented me on my cock sucking. The bastard saw it as a way to take a little more control. Jack wrenched his hard cock out of my throat and pulled it away from me. When I reached out to take it back, he held it up to stop me.

Jack leaned back on his desk and spread his legs wide, his pants hanging at his ankles. He started waving his big cock in my face.

"You really love cock, don't you Andrea?" he asked.

I moaned affirmatively as I slid the cock in and out of my wet mouth, but he continued to tease me. Every now and then, he would let the cock head drop on my thrashing tongue.

"You'd do anything to suck a hard cock, wouldn't you Andrea?" he queried.

I nodded that I would, and then held my head back and opened my mouth. Still not giving me what I needed, the fucker continued.

Rubbing the fiery hot cock over my cheek, he said "You'd even whore to get cock, wouldn't you?"

"Yes!" I yelled back, lunging for his cock.

Finally satisfied with my answer, Jack cupped the back of my head and guided the throbbing cock deep into my throat.

"Ahhhhh . . . you'd be a great whore," he said.

I willingly continued with my duty. This bastard was no cocksman, and I knew he would blow soon.

I could feel the cum starting to run. The next withdrawal of the cock head brought with it a long string of drool that ran from the head to my lips. I pulled my head back so Jack could see the long string.

I started to suck harder and harder, until I could feel Jack's ball sac tighten in my fingers. I rubbed them with my nails, driving him crazy with lust.

It was time to make him blow. I sucked the cock partly in my throat to finish the job, running my tongue out as I impaled myself on the shaft. I needed to ensure that the fresh load of cum would hit the mark.

Jack had others ideas.

Jack grabbed my head and abruptly yanked the cock out of my throat. He started to savagely jack off the throbbing stick. The head grew in size as he tightly hand fucked his cock. Suddenly, Jack commanded me in a hurried voice.

"Lean back, bitch," he said in an icy tone.

I continued to do as I was told. I leaned back and opened my mouth for him to fill it with his seed.

"Cum in my mouth" I swooned, looking into his eyes and waiting.

Jack grunted and moaned, jacking his cock wildly in front of my face. Suddenly and without warning, Jack re-aimed the cock head as the first blast flew, hitting me square in the forehead.

The cum started to gush. Another thick jet that landed in my hair, and two more that completely creamed by chin and neck. Jack had dumped his hot cum all over my face, and in no time it started to drip all down my face and chin.

I swear that I could feel the cum when it rolled over my pearl necklace and formed a puddle in my cleavage. I guess he gave me another pearl necklace!

I felt so decadent as this bastard spunked me up. My fingers reached out and my tongue started out to lap up the tasty wad on my chin. I was in heaven mixing it with my lipstick.

As I started to clean up his mess, Jack walked closer and started to wipe his cum chunks around my face with the tip of cock head, laughing.

"What a fucking slut," he ridiculed.

It was then that I realized what he was doing, that it was on purpose.

I was at work, a professional woman working in a large bank as an assistant manager. What would the customers and other employees think when the bastard threw me out of his office, my face and neck smothered in cum, globs hanging in my hair?

Sure enough, the son-of-a-bitch slipped his cock in his pants and briskly walked me to the door.

"Get the fuck out of here until I call for you," Jack said coldly.

I was mortified, stricken by not knowing how to avoid the inevitable embarrassment. What could I do? I couldn't let people see me!

I fumbled with the lock, unable to simply undo it because I was so shaken. I slipped out the door in dread that someone would see me. I carefully slinked off to the bathroom to clean up.

Thankfully nobody did notice.

Chapter 18

I sat in my office, waiting to be called in to sexually administer to the bastard I started to hate so much. This son-of-a-bitch was taking advantage of my womanly needs, using me like a cheap cum whore. To make matters worse, the bastard didn't even fuck me long enough so I could orgasm.

That afternoon the call came. I walked into Jack's office wondering if this episode would be any better. He looked up from his desk with a lecherous look on his face. The look on his face concerned me when he asked me to sit down.

"I need to talk to you," he said with a rather warm tone to his voice.

Oh no, I thought, now what?

"Have a seat," he said.

Jack got up and walked to the door as I sat down, shutting it as I had intentionally failed to do so. I think he locked it, too, but I couldn't see. He came back and sat in the chair next to me.

"Andrea, this situation can be good for both of us, don't you think?"

I just looked at him with surprise as he continued.

"You are obviously a very horny woman, and I won't lie to you," he said, "you're incredibly attractive."

Finally, a real compliment from the bastard.

Jack went on, leaning closer to me.

"So, I have a proposition to make," he said.

He slipped off his chair and kneeled in front of me.

"You know I'm married, and my wife is nothing like you," he told me.

"And . . ," I said.

"And . . . ," he said slowly as he started to rub his hand over my leg, "I think you and I should help each other take care of our needs here at work."

I remained silent, waiting to hear more.

Jack slowly moved his hands between my thighs, uncrossing my legs. He ran his two hands up my short dress. As he caressed me at the top of my stockings, the selfish bastard started to speak matter-of-factly.

"I'll give you cock every day Andrea, and no one has to know, he said.

He apparently had me pegged as a raving nymphomaniac.

"You'd like that, wouldn't you?" he asked.

Jack stopped rubbing my thighs, waiting for a response.

"What do you think?" he asked again.

"Well, Jack . . . I don't know," I started.

Jack didn't wait for me to complete my answer, instead lifting up my dress and prying my legs further apart.

"Your wife would be pretty . . . upset."

Jack responded by pushing my panties aside and thrusting his tongue into my gash. The sensation immediately broke down my resistance, much as it did when Bill did it – the last man to eat my cunt. Even Mark had eaten me in the last year.

As Jack wormed his tongue over my clit and into my hairy cunt, I instinctively started to rub my fingers through his hair.

"Ohhhh, God," I blurted out.

With that he knew he had me. Jack looked up at me with a lecherous smile as his finger worked over my clit.

"So we have a deal?" he asked.

"We'll see how it goes," I said.

I wondered if the fucker would be true to his word. If he would, it would solve my problems, at least for a while.

Jack then abruptly stood up before me. I expected the fucker to jam his cock in my face again. Instead, he took me by the hands and helped me to stand. He wrapped his arms around me and started to kiss me.

It was a rather passionate kiss. As Jack worked his tongue into my mouth, he reached around and fondled my ass. I pushed back when I felt his strong hands. I was led over to the couch that was in his office.

Jack gestured for me to sit down. I did so, and he quickly kneeled in front of me. Jack raised my dress to my waist. He pushed my thin panties to the side so my cunt would be exposed for his horny tool. He started to lick my gash some more.

"Ohhhh," I moaned as he licked and fingered me.

The cunt licking didn't last for long. In an instant, he pushed me over onto my back. Jack looked at me with those still cold eyes and lecherous look as he briskly unbuckled his pants and unzipped his zipper.

Jack said but one word.

"Spread."

I compliantly did so, submitting my open cunt for his use as he crawled up onto the sofa.

Jack kneeled between my legs, preparing to mount me. He swiftly pulled down his pants and underwear, allowing his turgid cock to spring free.

Without taking his eyes off from me, Jack moved closer between my legs me until his cock was at the entrance to my hole. His gaze fixed, he reached out and took me by the waist.

Ready to use my married cunt for his lecherous pleasures, Jack swiftly pulled my cunt onto his prick until I was fully impaled. When the cock head rapidly stretched open my cunt and came to a stop deep inside me, my mouth to popped open and a low, whorish groaned escaped from my lips.

The filthy office scene – and the feeling of the abrupt invasion of my cunt – caused my eyes to close and my head to fall back into the cushion.

"Mmmm . . . ," he said, "I love your sweet cunt."

I gave another whorish moan of approval in response.

"Ahhhh . . . fuck," I groaned, "fuck me hard, you bastard."

Jack then proceeded to really give it to me, lifting my legs and tossing them over his shoulders. He immediately began to stroke my soft cunt with a powerful long dicking, causing my heels to bang against his back.

Jack took his free hand and reached up my hiked dress, and started squeezing my big tits through my bra. The feeling was incredible, a new way of fucking for me.

I felt on the verge of cumming with each forceful lunge of the fiery hot cock. God, I wanted to get humped so bad! Unfortunately, I could feel the son-of-a-bitch's back stiffen.

Jack rammed his prick deep into me, and his head came down next to mine as he panted. The jets of hot cum started to pump into my hungry cunt as the bastard's outstretched tongue ran across my neck.

As the throbbing cock unload its seed, the bastard grunted in my ear.

"Ohhhhh fuck . . . I'll . . . feed . . . you cum . . . every . . . day, ahhh . . ."

So, here I was, giving into Jack and allowing him another afternoon fuck. I was so close, and the lousy bastard didn't even help me to cum.

I later thought about it, and based on the remark he made while shooting into me, I concluded that he was either selfish or incredibly stupid. Sure, I loved cum, but didn't the bastard realize that women orgasm too?

Yes, this was all very hard for me. I had a loving husband, but I was my asshole boss' unsatisfied mistress. Why?

Chapter 19

It was a strange relationship between Jack and myself. I needed the sex, I was desperate for it. The recurrent ache between my legs wouldn't let me forget that I was now a lady who needed to get laid on a regular basis.

And my poor husband. I was still putting off Mark the best I could, thinking that he would eventually be able to tell that I had succumbed to an untold number of cocks. So I couldn't get it at home, but I didn't want to tramp around either. But I never thought I'd be someone's mistress.

It was dilemma, and Jack seemed to be an acceptable solution. I figured that the worthless bastard was better than nothing, even though he had a little dick. He was safe because he was married too. Quite frankly, I didn't care if he used me as long as I got laid by a horny cock.

I eventually learned to take care of the orgasm problem. The bastard always came too fast! I found that rubbing my clit as I got laid usually did the trick. I just had to position myself so I could get my hand between my legs. Another problem solved!

Jack also made it clear without saying the words that he could make my job a lot easier as my lover. I must say, at least his wretched treatment of me came to an end.

In return for this special treatment, I was Jack's personal slut. I willingly administered to his sordid lust every day. This time around, however, I prepared.

Now that I was my boss's fuck toy, I made sure that I got on birth control. I didn't want a repeat of the deep feeling of anxiety and nervousness that I felt when my period was late last year. Yet another problem solved!

Office sex was the deal, and Jack wanted his deal! Like clockwork, Jack would call me in at 10:00 a.m. for a morning blowjob, and 2:30 p.m. for an afternoon fuck. It was always something exciting with him.

Some days when I was wearing a suit, I would unbutton my blouse and bra to let the dirty fucker tit fuck me and then splash hot cum all over my tits. Jack loved using his prick to wipe his sticky cum all over my tits when he was done shooting, and I loved feeling his hot cum on my skin.

Other times he have me suck him. When he was close to shooting, he would take my hands and turn them over. The sick bastard loved the look of my long, delicate fingers with their freshly manicured red nails. He really got off splashing cum all over my fingers, making sure that he buried my wedding ring in a huge gob of cum.

Whatever. I would always just bring my hand to my mouth and lap up the wad of cum like a hungry whore.

Jack also started teasing me during the day. Sometimes after our afternoon fuck appointment, he would come up to me in the main room and whisper things in my ear. Jack would tell me he was turned on knowing that I was working with customers with his seed being soaked up by my dress, or that he loved knowing I was working with a hairy cunt full of seed. God, the comments made me so fucking wet! I could hardly wait for our next fuck session!

I eventually learned to gauge my appearance by how fast the inconsiderate bastard came. It seemed that the better I thought I dressed and looked any particular day, the faster he came. I tested my theory one day by wearing pants. It was a little harder to drop them to accept his cock, but sure enough he took longer. Not long enough for me to cum without rubbing my clit, though.

I decided to make a point of wearing skirts and dresses. I loved getting fucked, but he started to avoid balling me whenever I wore slacks. Yes, I thought. Skirts and dresses so the fucker could feel me up. My wet, hairy cunt always did its job. Arousing the bastard until he stroked his cock between my legs!

Some days I would wear a sexy dress with nylons and perfume. I would pop into his office for a quick second, hike up my dress and show him my hair bush, rubbing my fingers between my cunt lips. On those days, we would get together afterwards and he shoot his wad on my lips after only one or two strokes! How I loved seeing how fast I could make this bastard cum!

Life was good. Work was now something I enjoyed going to, waiting in anticipation every morning for my daily screwing.

But as time went on, Jack pressured me for more. Jack tried like a bastard to talk me into fucking him after work. He was relentless. And I was insatiable. On those nights, I would tell my husband that I had to work late for an audit or whatnot. Jack and I would then fuck all evening in his office on the sofa in his office. It really is surprising that the janitors never heard us.

The trysts became more of a turn-on day after day. I became hornier and hornier. My lust appetite was growing out of control, my addiction to cum becoming uncontrollable. Every day at 10:00 and 2:30, I was there ready to give service . . . and to be serviced.

Jack's hot cock felt great, but deep down I knew that my needs just weren't being met. For starters, he wasn't an ass fucker, and I felt a need for a royal ass reaming. He also didn't have any stamina. My hot cunt was just too much for the lousy fuck. And I always felt guilty about Mark.

In reality, it was a bad situation. I didn't know how to handle my growing sexual needs. Jack just wasn't doing it for me any more. And my guilt kept increasing. I loved my husband so much, and I just wished our sexual relationship could be exciting.

This "arrangement" with Jack only went on for about two months, when something happened that did satisfy my needs . . . for a while. It was degrading as hell. And it taught me just how much of a prick Jack really was.

Chapter 20

A memo was sent around one afternoon informing us that the main office was sending an important potential customer to our office. All we were told was that he was a wealthy international businessman who wanted to see how the bank operated and to talk to the key managers.

The man was apparently from some oil producing nation in the Middle East. He was concerned with where he put his money in the United States, and he wanted to feel comfortable with his banking relationship.

Jack called me and told me that I would be having lunch with him and the visitor the next day. I knew that this was an important meeting. How we handled this customer would be important not only for the bank, but for my career. When I got up that day, I made sure that I looked the part of a professional banker.

Today, I selected a dignified yet sexy business suit. The suit consisted of a skirt that went down to my knees which hooked in the back. There was no blouse, but a jacket that buttoned up the front.

The jacket was admittedly low cut, but I thought it never hurts to show your cleavage when you've got it. Besides, I wore a simple bra that definitely covered my tits..

For underwear, I wore panties as usual, but today I decided on crotchless pantyhose as all of my stockings were in the wash. All I had was a pair of small black fishnet. What the hell I thought.

As usual, I wore a necklace and my wedding rings. A nice pair of high heels with an ankle strap finished it. My hair and makeup were perfect. Red nail polish and dark eye shadow as usual. A splash of perfume topped it off.

I went to work and met the customer. When he walked into the bank, I could tell that he was a rich foreigner just from the look of his suit. He was introduced to me and Jack by one of the vice presidents, who turned him over to us.

The businessman's name was Jamar. He was a tall, older man of about 55. He was clearly an Arab, I thought, from his dark brown complexion and thick accent. He had a pleasant, friendly personality. And he certainly liked me, judging from the way he looked me over!

I was surprised when Jack had another manager show Jamar around and answer his questions. It was something Jack would usually do himself, but the bastard was more interested in my daily 10:00 oral services.

Jack knew the lunch meeting was important, so I was relieved he was careful to make sure his cum ran down my throat and not on my clothes. At least he had some common sense, I thought.

Jamar was staying at a luxurious hotel in the city. We met Jamar at the hotel restaurant for the lunch meeting. Jack brought a thick stack of papers for his review and signature in order to get the banking relationship started.

Jack wasn't tactful. He immediately started to talk business as soon as we sat down. I could see that Jamar was not pleased. I looked at Jack and cut in.

"Why don't we get to know Jamar a little better before we get into that Jack," I said.

Jamar smiled, obviously pleased with what I said. He agreed, saying that he wanted to wait until after we ate before we discussed business.

We engaged in a lot of small talk while we ate. Everyone at the table was married and had children. We talked about our families, Jamar smiling at me the whole time. I just looked back at him and smiled, wanting to impress him so he would consider using our bank.

As lunch was progressing, I was stunned when Jamar reached under the table and ran his hand over my knee. At first I pushed his hand back, but the Arab kept attacking. Each time I moved his hand and put it right back.

Eventually, I just gave in. Who cared if this bastard copped a feel?, I thought. What harm would be done, especially if it helped to close the deal? My mind was made up, and I decided to let the prick go ahead and feel me up.

As soon as my defenses were down, Jamar started running his hand higher and higher, stroking my fishnet pantyhose. The Arab continued to work his way up my legs, I instinctively started spreading me legs to let him in.

Jamar caressed the skin of my thigh as he got to the top of my fishnets. It felt great, causing my legs to spread further. Soon he would find they were crotchless.

Jamar took advantage when I relaxed and let my guard down. His hand soon came to my pussy. His fingers brushed my panties aside, and soon he was running them through my pussy hair.

It was wild. Here I was sitting in an expensive restaurant on a business matter, the client stroking my bush. It have to say that it felt exciting getting felt up by a sophisticated, strange foreigner during a public lunch. I was getting wet, no doubt about it. Jamar loved it.

Jamar nonchalantly continued talking as he slipped a finger into my dripping pussy. He started stroking my cunt lips under the table, flicking his finger over my clit. He was driving me crazy, making my pussy so wet.

As Jamar worked another finger into my slit, I could feel my hips push up to invite his fingers into me. The whole time Jamar continued the conversation with me and Jack, never hinting at our secret.

At the end of the lunch, Jamar looked at me and announced to the table that he was feeling a bit tired. He asked if we would mind if we discussed business later that afternoon. Jack smiled at him, and then at me. Why was Jack so agreeable?

Jamar then stood up and announced that he was staying in the penthouse, in room 814. He then looked straight at me and said I was welcome to join him for a drink upstairs if I was free. He noticeably did not include Jack in the invitation.

Jamar got up and walked away without saying another word. I was stunned at the invitation. I looked at Jack with a look of disgust on my face.

"Presumptuous, asshole, isn't he?" I said.

It was then that I discovered what a lousy fucker Jack really was.

"Well, Andrea, maybe Jamar expects a little more for his money," he said slowly.

I looked at Jack with utter disbelief at what was unfolding.

"He's a very important customer for the bank," he went on, "keeping his accounts would really help my career and yours."

The import of his statement hit me like a ton of bricks.

"What did you say to him, Jack?" I demanded to know.

He looked at me with a stern look.

"Andrea, you told me you'd whore for cock, remember?" he asked.

He put his hand on mine and squeezed.

"Does it really matter who you put out for? You love getting laid by anybody."

I must admit that I had said it, but I said it in the heat of passion. It didn't occur to me that the bastard would take me up on it and set me up to fuck a client. How low did this asshole think I was?!?

I also had to admit the Jack was right. I loved to get laid, and God knows I was desperate to get laid by a real man. Who knows, maybe this exotic guy could finally satisfy my insatiable desires?

Jacked continued.

"And you let him feel you up during lunch, so it's not like I was wrong thinking you'd put out to him."

I was stunned again. Jack sensed my wonderment at his knowledge from the inquisitive look on my face.

"He told me when you went to the ladies room that you had beautiful legs," he said.

"He then asked me if you ever strayed on your husband."

"What did you tell him?" I demanded to know.

"I told him that you are available, that your marriage was open, and that you loved being with different men."

"Oh my God," I said, looking down at the table in disbelief. I couldn't believe it. That is why the Arab bastard took the liberty of feeling up this female bank manager he had met only hour before!

"Well, Andrea, I think it's true," he said in defense of himself.

"Bullshit, Jack," I said, "you're just whoring me to further your career."

Jack wasn't phased at my comment.

"You want to fuck him," he said, "admit it."

"No, Jack," I said, "I'm not a whore."

As attracted as I was to Jamar, and as much as I enjoyed the incredible feel job he gave me during lunch, this turn of events left me speechless and quite upset.

Jack continued trying to talk me into whoring for him.

"Come on, Andrea," he said, "I could probably get you a hefty raise if we get this guy to deposit a good chunk of his wealth in our bank. Well, if you let him deposit a good chunk of his wad in your tight cunt!"

There it was. The lousy, crass bastard really was whoring me to advance his career. I was so pissed., I was ready to scream.

But Jack was right. I had thought about what it would be liked to fuck Jamar when I met him. And his skillful finger job of my cunt! I was still wet. My body kept telling me that I may be able to get a good lay from the mysterious stranger.

My mind raced, and my hormones eventually convinced me. I'd do it. I'd see how it goes.

But this fucker, I thought, he needed to pay a hefty price himself.

"Fine, I said," getting up to do his bidding.

"I'll put out, but only if our relationship is over, Jack."

He was stunned.

"But Andrea . . .", he started to say.

"I'm sorry, Jack," I responded, "but you know I don't have multiple lovers. I just won't do that!"

And it was true. Other than my husband, Jack was my only lover.

Jack reluctantly agreed. Apparently his greed was more rampant than his lust.

As I started to walk away, something in me made me turn around. I grabbed a glass of water sitting on the table and splashed it in his face.

"You bastard," I shouted, as I quickly storming out of the dining room.

As I rode the elevator to the third floor, a sick feeling came over me. I couldn't believe Jack had done this. And I imprudently agreed to his plan of whoring me for the bank! My God, what would Mark say if he ever found out?!?

I considered just leaving, but I knew the client would not use our bank to hold his fortune if Jack's promise to him wasn't kept. And I really needed to keep my job. If he didn't get me fired, Jack would surely make life a living hell for if I did didn't honor my agreement.

Chapter 21

I rode the elevator to the third floor, adjusting my stocking and skirt as it went up. I walked up to room 814, mentally preparing myself to give the Arab his piece of American ass.

I reluctantly knocked on the door, and the deep voice came back.

"Come in Andrea," he said.

So presumptuous. He knew it was me.

The door was unlocked. I opened the door and walked into the room. The room looked like a palace. It had to be the most expensive room in town.

Jamar was sitting on a chair by the bed. He was in his undershirt, his dress shirt and tie already off. The burly Arab had a lecherous smile on his face. The bastard knew that I was there to submit to his sexual needs. I looked down, ashamed because I knew it too.

I stood before him and looked up. I didn't say a word, waiting for the command that I knew would come. I even thought he would jump me right there.

I was wrong.

"Andrea, I am so pleased you could join me," he said as he stood.

He walked over to a small bar in the room and asked me if I wanted a drink.

"Just some water, please," I said.

"Ah, a lady like you needs a real drink!" he said as he poured me some bourbon.

I took the drink as he smiled at me. I took a sip, knowing that me and strong alcohol didn't mix.

"You're an incredibly beautiful woman," he said softly.

"Thank you, Jamar," I responded.

He came close to me and looked down at me.

"Show me how beautiful you are," he ordered.

I instinctively went for the buttons on my blouse, thinking he wanted to see me naked.

"No, don't undress" he said, "just walk around."

The man wanted to appreciate my fine lines, so I turned and walked around the room a bit. I kept looking back at him, wondering what he would do next.

Jamar walked over to a chair as I walked around the room. He leaned over to a radio that was on a side table and turned it on. Soft music began to play.

"Dance for me, Andrea," he ordered as he turned on some music.

While I just wanted to give him piece of ass and move on, this horny bastard wanted to enjoy every minute with me. I danced around in front of him slowly, twirling and causing my hair to fly. I was starting to get aroused.

"Show me your beautiful legs," he commanded.

Enjoying the compliment and the fixed attention of my suitor, I kicked my leg and slowly raised my skirt high above my knee, giving a glimpse of my black fishnet stockings.

"Oh, so beautiful," he said softly.

As I ran my hands over my stockings, I could feel that they were wet. My pussy was dripping. I was so fucking excited!

I reached up and slowly unbuttoned the top two buttons of my jacket so he could see my cleavage a little better.

"Ahhh . . . you are so, so beautiful Andrea," he said.

To thank him for his compliment, I hiked my skirt up higher and pushed my panties to the side, exposing my hairy snatch. I ran my fingers through my bush, and then started rubbing the wetness of my cunt on my pink lips. I was a wanton woman on fire!

It was too much for the bastard to take.

Jamar gestured for me to come closer, waving his hand across his crotch. I knew what the bastard wanted, so I danced over to him and just fell to my knees.

I knew my job, to service his cock with my throat. I was ready and willing.

As I reached for his zipper, Jamar stopped me with his next command.

"Take off my shoes, Andrea," he instructed.

I felt like a cheap whore as I reached back and untied his shoes. As I slipped them off, he commanded me again.

"Now my pants," he said coldly.

I reached up and unbuckled his pants.

As I unsnapped the top and drew down the zipper, he gently caressed my hair. I reached to his waist and yanked. He smiled as he lifted his ass, allowing me to get them down.

"And now my underwear."

I looked at the bulge in his pants, quite large from what I could see. I again reached up for his waist, and pulled his underwear off.

I was shocked yet delighted that his big brown cock was so large. God, I had never seen a cock of this color. I was mesmerized.

Jamar reached behind me and cupped the back of my head, quickly drawing it into his groin.

The depraved Arab thrust my head onto his prick and nestled by nose under his musty balls. My tongue leapt from my mouth and I started to work it over the hairy ball sac.

I reached up with my hand to cup his incredibly heavy balls, reaching up to stroke the wakening snake with my other hand. In no time his hot prick was as stiff as a board, ready to be serviced. The man certainly got horny feeling me up at lunch.

I gazed in wonderment at the incredible thing. His bone hard cock had to be as long and thick as Al's, perhaps even a little larger. I had no idea an Arab could be so hung. No wonder they needed harems!

I didn't care. I was just happy that God blessed me with a hung stud to fill my wet snatch.

I sucked the Arab stud's stiff prick into my hungry mouth, my inhibitions being freed by the sight of the meaty fuck stick. I was actually salivating, drooling down on the beautiful Arab cock.

I licked Jamar's cock up and down, jacking it each time I popped the throbbing mushroom head into my mouth. This went on for about five minutes as the lecherous Arab bastard moaned in delight.

I wanted more. I popped the monstrous stick into my mouth to see if I could take in my throat as easily as I had been taking Jack all these months. Jamar was a lot larger than Jack, however, and my throat was no longer accustomed to such a large pole.

Jamar appreciated what I was doing. He had no intention of letting me fail.

"Ah yes, Andrea," he cooed, "take me into your mouth!"

I tried several times to work the fuck stick into my throat, but I could only get it about half way in. On my last attempt, Jamar grabbed the back of my head and forced me down on his cock.

I started to gag from the size, trying desperately to remember Bill's warning to relax.

The depraved fucker still didn't stop, intent on choking me to death if I did not accept his blood engorged tool. What a ruthless stud, I thought.

Jamar pushed harder and harder, and I started to squirm.

I put my hands on his legs and tried to pull up. Jamar just pushed that much harder. Thankfully my throat started to give, and soon my fully stretched mouth was fully impaled by the Arab's big cock. I could feel the massive cock head firmly lodged deep in the back of my throat, throbbing in a deep lust. I tried desperately to breath, and my body flailed.

I went to withdraw the enormous tool, but I felt myself pinned down by Jamar's hand. He would not let me up yet.

I focused on just trying to breath, even though my nose was buried in the Arab's thick patch of pubic hair. I finally managed to calm myself, remembering what Bill had taught me.

A few seconds later, Jamar grabbed my head. He roughly wrenched my throat from his cock until my lips were at the tip of the massive cock head. I caught my breath as fast as I could.

I was ready to tell Jamar what a fucker he was for the brutal way he mouth fucked me, but he swiftly pushed my head back onto the thick shaft before I had a chance.

Jamar brutally fucked my throat like this for a good ten minutes. By the time he was done, my throat readily accepted his ruthless moves.

My passions arose during those ten minutes like they never had before. Memories of the fateful day returned, and I knew I was in the hands of another old stud.

With the last wrenching of his cock from my throat, Jamar looked at me with cold eyes and told me to unbutton my blouse. Kneeling before him, I did as I was told, until the suit jacket fell open.

I reached behind and unsnapped my bra.

My large, firm tits sprang free.

"Ahhh . . . such tits," he said coldly.

"Hold them together for me," he ordered.

I cupped my tits and rubbed them for him. I then squeezed them together as I tweaked my nipples. Jamar wormed his body down as I put on my show.

"Come closer," he said.

Jamar started working his fat cock between my tits. He held me by the shoulders and I held my tits together. He worked his prick between my tits, obviously loving the tit fucking.

I must admit that it aroused me greatly knowing the huge Arabian stud was getting such joy from rubbing his massive cock against my tits. The more he used me, the more I wanted to service this stud.

Jamar did this for a few minutes before ordering me to stand up.

I got up off from my knees stood before him. My jacket was open, my bra was hanging down, and my tits exposed.

Jamar then stood up and savagely pulled off my jacket and bra. He quickly took me in his strong arms, his massive hard-on jammed into my crotch.

As he licked my neck, I could feel his erect pecker poking into my cunt. My skirt was between us, and I was aghast to see a long string of pre-cum dribbling from his cock and down the front.

Jamar ground his cock harder into me, grabbing my ass and pulling my body towards it. He fiercely kissed me as he dry-humped me like a dog.

It felt great as our tongues rolled together, the huge prick pushing against my skirt. The bastard was so strong. I just stood there with my mouth wide open, letting the depraved fucker lick the inside of my mouth.

Jamar then went back to licking my neck, every so often grabbing my and squeezing tits with a deep moan.

The Arab was a master stud. He eventually reached behind me and unsnapped my skirt, letting it fall to the floor. Jamar stopped and wrapped his arm around my waist. He pulled me tightly to him, reaching down for my leg with his free hand.

I could feel the brute as he grabbed my leg and jerked it up, resting my foot on the chair by the bed. He then reached down and pulled up my slip, firmly holding it at my waist with his hand.

Jamar looked me straight in the eye as his big cock head started probing between my legs, intent on inserting his huge rod between my spread legs. His hands and arms used to pin me tight, his body writhed until the cock could find my cunt on its own.

Suddenly, the cock head found its mark. It started to push into me.

I could feel the stiff prick as it pierced my pink cunt lips. This was the biggest cock head I had experienced in over a year. My eyes opened wide and a whorish moan came out of my mouth to betray my final submission to the Arab brute.

Jamar pushed his cock into me, pulling closer to him by my waist. My cunt slowly spread open to accept the massive cock head, my lusty groans clearly exciting the lecherous bastard.

As Jamar split me open, the fucker looked at me and moaned. He was soon in balls deep, my cunt stretched wide apart to accommodate the giant fuck stick.

I was laid.

As my cunt snapped shut on his horny thick cock, Jamar held me close and savored the feeling of his thick cock lodged so deep inside of me. The Arab's fiery hot cock just throbbed deep in my cunt. I could literally feel how hot the prick was!

Jamar then reached behind me to insert a finger into my ass, which caused a sensation that pushed me further over the edge. Another whorish moan escaped from my lips as he worked his finger in and out of my ass!

Jamar then began his fucking.

I stood there with my leg up on the chair as the stud started to slow fuck me, my cunt viciously pulling on his cock as he tried do so. He got my body to help him by pulling me close to him with the finger he had stuck in my ass. I have to say, it was a new sensation to be fucked like this!

Putting more force into the task, Jamar wretched his cock from my tight cunt and jammed it back in. I knew I was about to get drilled by that massive Arab cock.

Once Jamar was warmed up and my cunt was nice and wet for him, he proceeded to pound me. He drove his tool in and out of me with swift, brutal strokes, my cunt loosening to accommodate the angry hard tool.

It was no time before the stud had me cumming. All I could do was moan as I stood there, being savagely taken by this Arab brute. Each time he deep stroked me, I moaned loudly from the deep roguish fucking this sex starved animal was giving me.

Jamar enjoyed the show. He would look down with pride to see his big cock working its way through my married American cunt.

"Ah . . .".," he said.

"You are so tight, Andrea!!!!!"

Jamar fucked me like that for about five minutes, causing me to orgasm again. And then, without warning, he withdrew his tool and grabbed me by the arms.

I was startled by the stud's action, and more so when he literally threw me face first onto the bed. I lifted myself slightly by my elbows and looked behind to see what Jamar was going to do next, my legs slightly spread from the force of being thrown on the bed.

Jamar quickly climbed on the bed and moved between my legs. He rapidly hiked up my slip and mounted me from behind in one swift stroke. The feeling of the massive hot prick being forcefully jammed up my cunt caused me to cum again.

"Ahhh . . . Ohhh . . . ," he heard me groan.

"Oh God, please don't stop!"

Once firmly imbedded deep in my cunt, Jamar continued the brutal fucking. He hammered my cunt mercilessly, sweating and grunting the whole time. I could feel my legs tremble as he started to ride me like a whore.

And then he startled me again.

The stud withdrew and then pushed me over on my side. He rolled me over and lifted my legs. The crawled between my legs to mount me again. Jamar put his strong arms around my neck and began long dicking me with his thick cock.

I was as horny as I had ever been, and I ground my heels into the bed so I could push back to meet his thrusts. It was the wonderful, hard fucking that I so desperately needed from a huge, thick cock! I was ecstatic, crying out when I had another orgasm as the bastard savagely took me with that incredible dong of his.

"Fuck me, you bastard, fuck my hot cunt," I begged.

When the stud heard those words, he went nuts. Jamar lifted my legs as high as he could, until my ankles were literally behind by my neck. My cunt was up by my tits, and I felt totally opened to accept cock.

Jamar then stood above my cunt and proceeded to give me the fucking of my life, slamming his massive cock into my cunt with brutal force. I felt like a pin cushion for a steaming hot prick that stretched me over and over as he withdraw the huge cock and slammed it back into me. The sensation was incredible.

Each of Jamar's deep strokes drove the cock head so deep into me, I thought I was experiencing another womb fuck like Alvin had given to me. I was uncontrollably cumming over and over, praying that this deep fucking wouldn't stop.

Jamar grunted and groaned as he gave me this fucking, each thrust fully impaling me on his giant fuck rod. I could hear his giant ball sac as it slapped against my crack. And my cunt. It felt so wonderfully stretched by the massive girth of the hot prick.

The intensity of everything was so much, I could barely move. But Jamar knew the affect his cock was having on me by the constant whorish moans coming from me.

"Ahhhhhhhhh . . . . ," I moaned loudly each time his enormous cock head banged home.

"Ahhhh, your . . . cock . . . big . . ."

The whorish moans only enticed him to give it to me harder.

What an Arabian stallion!

A big cocked Arabian stallion!

My legs were numb by the time Jamar was finally finished using my pussy to work off his big prick. It must have lasted well over thirty minutes.

I knew the time was near when Jamar's pace slowed. The deep strokes turned into slow, long thrusts. With each new thrust, he slammed my cunt deep and exceptionally hard, the sign of a man ready to blow.

Sure enough, his back stiffened.

The cock pierced deep into my cunt, the balls as tight to my body as possible.

And then the jets of steamy hot cum started to blast all over my ovaries. The Arab grunted and groaned as he shot his wad deep into me. I could feel it. I could feel the thick prick as it stiffened and shot itself off, the hot wad scalding the inside of my pussy.

"Ahhh, fuck . . . Andrea . . . ahhhh . . ."

"Oh God," I moaned back, "your cum is so hot!"

I could literally feel stream after stream of the Arab's thick seed shoot against the insides of my well-fucked cunt. It was as though his balls were exploding inside of me. I was surprised as the throbbing cock kept pumping what had to be a tremendous load of cum, causing it to leak out of my cunt.

When the last jet finished, there was no doubt horny bastard had thoroughly painted my insides with his hot cum.

What a fucking stud! My dream stud!

I was in love! A deep, lusty love!

As soon as the last stream blew into my uterus, the bastard quickly dismounted and flopped on his back. Thinking I was done, I started to get up.

Jamar wasn't quite done with me yet.

Jamar grabbed me by the hair, and pushed my head down by his groin. I thought the fucker wanted me to clean off his pole with my tongue. Not yet.

The sadistic stud held my head between his legs, saying only two words.

"Let's rest."

He wasn't done using me.

Chapter 22

I laid there with my head between Jamar's groin for about twenty minutes as I regained my composure. I was dressed only in a slip, crotchless fishnet pantyhose, and heels. I felt like a pure whore, and I loved it.

I wondered what would be next. He was such a depraved fucker, I thought. I knew I was there to administer to his lecherous genitals, so I raised my hand to the hairy ball sac that my nose was nestled on. I rubbed it gently with my long nails.

"Ahhhh . . . ," he moaned.

Having received this sign of encouragement, I reached up and took his slick rod in my hand. I gently ran my nails over the soft rubbery skin as I started to jerk the cock back to life.

"Ohhhhh . . . ," he moaned as he started to rub his fingers through my long hair.

"Ahhh . . . Andrea!"

I did this for a few minutes, alternating the soft touch of my nails between his massive ball sac and jerking the gorgeous cock. I ran my tongue over the massive cock head as I serviced him this way.

The taste and smell of his balls was magnificent, and every so often I would rub my finger over his asshole to show my appreciation. To add to his excitement, I also started to pull myself up, rubbing my big soft tits up and down his awakening cock.

It took about fifteen minutes of handjob, fingering, and tit service before his cock was rock hard again. It was a sign that his next orgasm would be long in coming.

Once the brown prick was rock hard, it was my cue to orally service the filthy bastard with my mouth. I rolled on my stomach between his spread legs and held the huge fuck stick so it was sticking straight up in the air. I couldn't help but notice that I had drool running down from my lips to the thick cock head!

My body was telling me that I was hungry for hard cock, so I deep throated the fucker. I freely impaled myself on the long fuck stick as deep as I could. God did I love deep throating a huge cock!

As soon as the cock head was again lodged in my throat, Jamar grabbed my head and began gyrating his hips into my face. I repeatedly deep throated the cock in faster motions while continuing to rub his heavy balls with my nails.

Another twenty minutes and a sore throat later, Jamar raised his legs and sat up on the side of the bed. I followed him with my head, turning on the bed so I could take his pole in my mouth again. He stroked my long hair against my shoulders as I sucked on his cock some more, only to break the silence with his next command.

"Take off your slip."

I got up off the bed and stood right in front of him. I inserted my fingers into the elastic waistband and pushed the slip to the floor.

Jamar appreciated the sight, a thin naked woman wearing only crotchless fishnet pantyhose and high heels, a thick black hairy bush between her legs. He must have thought I was a real cock whore. And I was!

He reached around to fondle my ass, asking an unexpected question.

"You are married?" he asked, although he already knew it from our lunch discussion.

"Yes," I responded sheepishly.

"Your husband is a lucky man," he responded, as he ran his tongue over my stomach.

Jamar didn't really care. He turned me around so my back was to him, telling me to take him. I squatted down and grabbed his turgid pole with my hand, and gently eased my cunt onto the huge mushroom that waited under my cunt.

As I settled on the Arab's massive cock head and prepared to take the shaft, Jamar suddenly grabbed my waist and plunged me all the way onto his stiff prick. The feeling of the invasion caused my mouth to gape open and my head to fall back onto his shoulder. A sluttish groan escaped from me.

Jamar reached in front of me so he could rub my tits as I started to fuck him. He rubbed my heavy tits softly, tweaking my nipples every few seconds. As Jamar enjoyed my tits, my head turned on his shoulder to face him. He looked at me and we began to kiss as I humped up and down on his giant cock.

We both started to moaned uncontrollably, the sound of a stud with his whore. Our tongues rolled feverishly as he rubbed my tits faster, both of us enjoying the feeling of his motionless stiff cock stuffed deep inside my tight cunt.

"Andrea, I could keep my cock inside you forever," he said passionately.

"Mmmmmmmm . . ." was all I could say.

Again Jamar acted without warning. He stopped rubbing me and whispered in my ear to stand up.

I pulled myself self off from this cock and stood up, to be greeted by the feel of his hands on my ass cheeks. He quickly split my cheeks with his strong hands, and pulled my ass down onto his cock.

Clearly being another master cocksman, Jamar expertly positioned his cock head at the entrance of my asshole. When I felt his hands on my cheeks and the head at my ass, I knew what was going to happen.

I gasped as he pulled my ass harder onto his cock, and moaned loudly when the head broke through my tight hole. My ass could not be as tight as it had been before

Bill and Al, I thought, so I did not object as Jamar pulled my ass onto his cock.

It was such a long time since so many men had opened me, though my ass had tightened to a degree. That didn't stop Jamar. He wanted to fuck my white, married ass. Nothing would stop him.

The feeling was overwhelming as Jamar pulled me onto the huge pole, my asshole being split in two as the cock worked its way in. Jamar was clearly enjoying buttfucking me.

"Aggggh . . . please . . . no!" I groaned in pain.

I felt the overwhelming pain come back, but Jamar didn't care. He just brutally pulled me harder onto his massive prick.

"Agggggggh . . . no!" I groaned again.

My head flew back onto his shoulder again and my mouth gaped open. I knew begging wouldn't stop this depraved Arab bastard.

"Aggggggggh . . . Fuck," I muttered as the anal assault continued.

Halfway inside me, Jamar paused for a moment to savor the feeling of his throbbing cock being squeezed by my tight ass. He was impassioned with my deep, throaty moans, however, and began to pull me even harder onto him.

"Nggggggggh . . . God . . . fuck!" I screamed.

Jamar was soon joined by my own deep lust, and I grit my teeth and I thrust the rest of my remaining asshole onto his cock in a lustful submission.

"Ahhh Andrea . . . I've impaled you," he bragged with his thick accent.

His statement drew another whorish moan from within me, and he reached around to rub my tits some more. I reached back and fondled his hairy nut sac. Instinctively, I turned my head to let him kiss him again as I spoke.

"I want your cock to shoot in my ass," I moaned at him.

The sounds of a stud with his whore returned as we kissed, loud enough for anyone on the floor to hear.

Jamar broke our kiss by grabbing my ass and lifting it off from his cock. As soon as he was out with the exception of the big head, he savagely slammed my ass back onto his cock adding a few simple words.

"Make me cum!"

"Aggggh . . . fuck," I cried out again and again as he kept doing it over and over. Pulling me off from his cock, and slamming me back down on it.

The brutal Arab cocksman did this about ten times, each one causing me to groan in disbelief of the sensations I was feeling.

Intent on making me feel every inch of his throbbing hard cock, the dirty fucker wanted me to know just how much my cock stuffed asshole belonged to him at that moment.

Jamar finally stood up, his huge fuck stick still jammed deep into my ass. Cupping my tits, he started to walk forward. I could barely walk with Jamar's huge pole stuck in my ass, but he pushed me forward by the waist.

The depraved fucker must have enjoyed the sensation of walking with his gigantic bone stuffed in my asshole, but I soon saw that he was turning me around towards the bed. Jamar and I stood by the side of the bed. He slammed my face onto the bed, and firmly gripped me by the waist.

As I reached between my legs to rub my clit, he proceeded to long dick my ass with strong, brutal strokes, each one fully impaling me. With each stroke he withdrew his massive cock completely much like Al had, and then steamrolled the rock hard pole back into me.

Jamar ass reamed me continuously for at least ten minutes, bringing me to multiple orgasms as I moaned like a whore. But my knees buckled from standing there, and my head bent over to the bed.

The bastard was so intent on reaming my asshole that he didn't notice my imminent collapse. My knees gave way, and my pelvis slammed into the bed with one of his powerful strokes. The filthy bastard was giving me a savage ass fucking, though, and he didn't stop for an instant.

I reached onto the bed and grunted as I clawed my way onto it, the whole time with the big Arab on my back stroking my asshole like an animal in heat. I laid flat on the bed, my face stuck in the sheets, moaning from the intense buttfucking.

Jamar went on, reaming and reaming with his fiery hot cock. I myself was out of control when I started telling him what I wanted.

"Give me your thick cock, you bastard," I groaned.

"Stuff my asshole with your hard cock."

Eventually my vile statements caused him to lose control too. Jamar lifted my ass by the waist so he could take longer strokes. He ruthlessly slammed my tender ass, each stroke grinding my face harder into the bed.

After what must seemed like an hour of deep ass fucking, Jamar started blowing his wad deep in my ass, screaming out in some Arabic language.

When Jamar was done shooting, we both collapsed. Jamar panted as he laid on top of me, his cock still stuck deep in my ass.

After a few minutes the prick had softened, and Jamar pulled it out with a vengeance. He rolled over, pulling me up to lay next to him.

My back was to his chest, and he wrapped his arm over me. We both feel asleep rather quickly.

Chapter 23

Jamar slept in a half groggy state, his lecherous hands constantly working their way over my chest, tits and legs. Occasionally his big hands would grope between my legs, which I would instinctively spread to allow him to feel me up as he desired.

This sleepy rubbing and stroking lasted for over an hour, when I had to get up to go and relieve myself. I cleaned up as best I could when I was in the bathroom, and then slipped back onto the bed next to my lover.

Jamar perked up and started to talk as I crawled back onto the bed.

"You are such a beautiful woman," he started, rubbing my tits and legs with more energy.

"Thank you," I responded politely.

Jamar then lifted himself on his elbow and kissed my neck. It was rapidly becoming apparent that the filthy bastard still wasn't finished with me.

"I have never taken a woman like you," he went on chauvinistically.

"I can tell by your frenzied passion that you are natural lover," he complimented me.

"Thank you," I again responded.

I moved my hand to find his resting on my tit. I don't know why, but I gently caressed the pig's hand.

"I could sell a woman like you for a great deal of money," he quietly whispered.

I was shocked by the revelation, never having believed the stories we hear about white slavery. When I started to voice my objection, he went on.

"Men would enjoy you night and day," he said as he reached between my legs to cup my pussy with his strong hand.

His hand movements drew a sluttish moan from my lips.

"Your only role in life would be to service all of them however they asked," he told me as he felt me up.

I moaned again and he squeezed my bush, more for his touch than for his vile statement. Without waiting for more of a response from me, Jamar rolled me on my back and brought his mouth to mine.

Jamar kissed me deeply, and then stopped briefly to ask me a question.

"You would like that, wouldn't you?" he asked.

I was somewhat excited at the wicked thoughts he was placing in my mind, but I knew I could do those things here without literally being someone's fucking slave.

I told Jamar that I enjoyed my life here. I added for good measure that my husband has already bought me.

"I am already owned," I said.

Jamar laughed, being able to appreciate the sick side of the statement.

"Then why are you here?" he asked.

I was quick to come up with a response that I thought he would understand.

"My husband appreciates my value," I told him with a smile.

"And he wants me to enjoy myself . . . not so much for others, but for myself."

My husband did appreciate my value, but certainly not in this context! Oh God, if he only knew!

Jamar kissed me again, telling me that he also appreciated my value. He told me what a wonderful lover I was. He then told me about his wife, and how he came to marry her in some kind of pre-arranged marriage. He was comparing me to her, I guess. It was no wonder the fucker was so depraved.

Jamar then asked how much my husband charged for my services! What a fucking sexist pig, I thought!

The line of conversation was becoming twisted, and I had to end it before I was dragged off against my will. I abruptly told him that my husband does not charge for me, but freely gives me to men for an afternoon of pleasure when the situation suits his fancy.

Jamar again laughed, apparently knowing of some analogy from his native land.

"Well, then, I am glad that I suited his fancy."

The talking and kissing was clearly exciting Jamar, his stiffening hard-on starting to twitch over my belly. He kissed me again, grinding his cock against me and rubbing his hand over my bush.

When Jamar reached a finger in between my legs, I spread for him. He was soon working three of his large fingers into my cunt, kissing me the whole time.

Jamar reached under my back and picked me up with his strong arms. He took my leg and guided it over him. Sensing what the bastard wanted, I raised myself over his stiff cock. I grabbed the shaft and ground my pussy down onto it with one swift, sloppy push.

"Show me your value," he said sternly.

I placed my hands on his hairy chest, and raised my ass. I started to plunge up and down on his big brown cock, squeezing my cunt shut on it each time I impaled myself.

Jamar rubbed my tits, which were inches from his face, grunting his satisfaction with each down stroke.

After a few minutes Jamar closed his eyes and reached back to grab my ass cheeks. He started lifting my ass, slamming me down mercilessly on his hard pole. Jamar fucked me like than for about fifteen minutes, when he rolled the two of us onto our sides.

The Arab beast looked into my eyes and kissed me again, stroking his cock in and out of me with quick rapid movements. He then stopped and told me to raise my leg so he could watch what his cock was doing to me.

I did as I was told, and raised my leg straight up in the air.

Jamar placed his strong hand under my leg to help it stay up, and gazed down to watch his big cock pound me.

A few minutes later he rolled me again, this time flat on my back. He lifted himself up with his hands, and slowly worked his cock through my cunt. I though this was going to be another hour fucking, but he eventually stiffened his back. I was ready to accept his load.

I thought Jamar was going to cream between my legs again, but this time he surprised me by pulling out his prick and bringing it to my tits. Jamar jacked his cock over me, rubbing the stiff pole around my tits. He did this for about a minute when his face started to contort.

The Arab grunted and moaned, and soon a wad of cum was being shot between my cleavage and onto my tits. A puddle of cum pooled between my swollen tits.

The fuck master fell back on the bed and reached over to my tits. He rubbed his fingers in his cum and massaged it into my tits.

I found that there was little cum, because he had already blown two loads. I was sadly disappointed when he only brought his finger to my lips twice. But I licked his fingers off like a true cum slut, but I didn't want to upset this brute by asking for more.

When Jamar was done, I laid back and rested. I fully expected a third round of fucking from the horny foreigner.

Chapter 24

I was exhausted from the experience, feeling like such a whore for having put out so willingly to the depraved bastard. My mind kept racing back to Mark. What was I doing? How could I???

I thought Jamar was finished with me when he eventually got up off the bed to get cleaned up. I just laid on the bed thinking incessantly about the experience.

But I was wrong.

He wasn't done with me.

Jamar called for his driver to come and get his bags as he dressed. The driver was there in no time, so I reached for the bed spread and covered myself when Jamar let him in.

The driver was a huge Arab, someone Jamar apparently brought with him wherever he went. I could tell he was a brute, even though he was wearing a suit. His chest was bulging and his arms were muscular under the sleeves. Wow!

Jamar was finishing up and the driver waited for him. I was embarrassed that the driver waited by staring down at me. I guess you don't see the sight of a beautiful naked woman much in the Middle East.

Jamar came out, ready to go. He saw his driver staring at me and asked him a question.

"Do you like my American slut?" he asked his driver.

I was shocked at his language, and also by his pronouncement of ownership of me. Who did this bastard think he was?

I quickly realized that I was no more than a whore to this ruthless man, and that he meant it when he said he would love to sell me.

The driver nodded his approval to Jamar and then answered in a foreign tongue.

"Take her, I'll wait," Jamar responded.

My mouth fell open.

I have never dreamed something like this was possible. I was jolted by the offer Jamar so boldly made, and it took me a second to realize what was happening.

I went to get off the bed, but the driver was faster. In a flash he threw the cover off from me and was on the bed, climbing over me to straddle my body. I squirmed to pull myself out from the brute, but he was too big and strong.

The more I squirmed, the quicker I realized that I could not stop from being conquered by the new Arab stud. I laid back, accepting what was about to come.

Jamar sat in the chair right next to the bed as the driver forced himself on me, accepting the offer his boss so generously made. The driver held my squirming body down with his weight, and forced my legs apart. He got between them and quickly unbuckled his pants.

"Ah, fresh tight American cunt," he said as he jerked down his pants.

Little did he know I wasn't so tight anymore. I quickly saw that it didn't matter to him.

It all happened so fast. Before I knew it, the driver's stiff Arab prick popped out before my face.

The angry prick stuck straight out, looking for its natural resting place, a tight soft cunt. As I looked at his rod, I realized that my pussy might very well be tight for this bastard.

I looked longingly on this gorgeous man as he proceeded to mount me. Another well hung Arab stud with huge giant balls.

Seeing this man fight so hard to get a piece of me, and knowing that I would soon be getting force fucked was too much for me. Again, something snapped inside of me.

I knew at that point that I truly did exist to service hard cock. I didn't resist as the Arab pried my legs further apart with his strong hands, preparing to lay me.

In one powerful stroke, I was laid. The driver swiftly jammed his prick up my cunt, causing a deep, whorish moan to escape me. My body fell limp as I felt the huge fuck stick throb between my legs. Yes, I freely submitted to the brutal fucking.

I wrapped my legs around the brute and locked them tight. I drove my heels into his back as hard as I could as he furiously pounded my cunt with his hot cock.

Each animalistic grunt from the stud drew an equally intense sluttish moan from me. This was a man who handed gotten laid in some time, I thought. And I was the American slut who his boss gave him to be serviced.

Jamar loved the show. I glanced over to him periodically to see his reactions. He sat there with a wide grin on his face.

"Ah Andrea, I love to watch you get fucked!" he said.

I moaned as he said that, locking my eyes with his as I pushed back to meet his driver's thrusts.

"I appreciate a true whore!" he added.

The words set me off.

I continued to fucking the bastard, hoping for an orgasm for myself before he shot his wad. But Jamar wasn't done with his offers.

"She has a very tight ass, too," Jamar remarked to the driver.

The driver didn't need any more encouragement. He broke the lock of my legs around his back and pushed my legs over my head. He held them back as far as he could by tightly holding my ankles.

The Arab stud withdrew his rock hard cock from my cunt and aimed it at my still gaping asshole. The sides of my anus were deeply indented, showing the brutal ass fucking it had recently taken from Jamar's huge cock. It was now ready to service his driver's cock too.

The driver let his horny cock bob around my gaping asshole. He would push and try to get it in, but he always missed. So he released one of my ankles so he could hold his cock at my ass. I kept the leg up, resting it on his shoulder as he entered me. It must have been one hell of a decadent sight for Jamar,

As he had done with my cunt, the driver took my ass with one powerful, swift stroke. He placed the head at my asshole and pushed. The huge fuck stick was jammed up my ass in a flash.

Jamar laughed as the driver began to savagely fucked me up the ass, grunting and sweating like a horny animal as I cried out for more cock.

The stud stroked my ass for about 5 minutes. My feeling of my tight as was eventually too much for him. Soon his back was starting to stiffen, a sign Jamar also picked up on. The driver seemed intent on shooting in my ass, but Jamar had other ideas.

"I want you to cum on her face," Jamar commanded to his driver. Not surprising, since Jamar had miserably failed to spunk me up when he tried.

The driver took a few more strokes deep in my ass, and then abruptly wretched his big prick from my ass. He moved up to again straddle my chest, pinning my legs up by my neck with his knees.

Holding his fuck stick over my face, he stroked it a few times and the cum started to pour. He was a man who truly had not cum in some time.

The stud dumped massive chunks of hot cum all over my pinned face, grunting deeply as he did so. My face must gave been covered, as I could feel the scalding cum burning into my entire face as he used his cock head to push it into my open lips. God, I absolutely loved the feel and taste of the cum this man gave to me!

Yes, I wanted this brute's cum, and I wanted it NOW. I sucked on the driver's cock head as he slipped it into my mouth. I sucked the cock into my mouth and polished it off. When he withdrew, I slipped my tongue out to find a huge wad on my chin. I mixed it with my lipstick to savor the exotic taste I had come to love so much.

As I licked and swallowed, the driver jumped off the bed and zipped up his pants in a flash. As soon as the fucker was off from me, I brought up my fingers to help collect more cum from around my face, watching as a large string of cum stuck between my hand and my chin.

As I ran my fingers over the rest of my face to collect more cum, I noticed how the thick strings of cum I pulled from my face made my fingers look like they were webbed.

I decadently brought each finger to my mouth to voraciously suck the cum off. I was so intent to eat this hot cum, I barely noticed when Jamar and his driver got up to leave. I probably wouldn't have noticed either, had they not been laughing.

As I licked and savored the salty cum, Jamar said more to degrade me in a twisted, complimentary way.

"Andrea, you are a cum slut, I see. A woman who loves the taste of cum!"

"Ummm . . ." I said as I feverishly licked up the sticky wad.

As I continued to lick the cum off of my fingers, Jamar made an offer that surprised me.

"I promise you, I will give you all of the cum you can drink and money you can spend if you will become my assistant, my whore."

"You can call me any time," he then said, "now that I have an account with your bank."

So my performance got us the account, I thought. I was a decadent bitch who whored for the bank, but I loved every minute of it.

Jamar didn't wait for an answer from me. He simply walked out. The driver followed his employer out the door like a loyal dog who was just fed a treat.

My mind was spinning. I could make so much money and have all of the cock I could ask for.

But I loved my husband and family so much.

I leaned over in the bed to find Jamar's card on the side table. An invitation.

I rolled over and looked at myself in the mirror. What a mess!

The driver left gobs of cum in my messed up hair and all over my forehead. I had apparently missed it when I was seeking out the cum. Even my lipstick was still shiny from the cum that had run over my lips. I truly looked like a well used whore.

My cunt and ass were satisfied for the time being, as was my lust for cum as I gathered the remnants from my hair and forehead. I felt so low as I desperately pulled the cum out of my hair, but I wanted every drop I could possibly get. I vacuumed them into my mouth.

As I got out of Jamar's bed, I knew my asshole had to be bleeding. It had been a year since my ass was savagely taken by so many men on that only day I had ever been ass fucked. And I remember how my rectum was bleeding when I woke up the next day.

The pain Jamar caused me today was intense, and these brutal Arab bastards had ruthlessly ass fucked me for over an hour with their huge cocks! I looked down on the sheets, and sure enough. A small pool of blood. I looked at my skirt, and I saw some more dried blood stains.

I went into the bathroom and washed the blood off as best I could. I took a quick shower to soothe my aching ass. And then I put on my lipstick and got dressed.

As I started to leave the building, I decided to go to the hotel bar. It was late enough, and happy hour was going on. I just wanted to see just how sexy I was. I certainly felt sexy, having gotten repeatedly laid the past few hours.

Sure enough, at least six handsome men came up to me to talk. One black man in particular interested me so much. His name was Tony.

I couldn't help but wonder how big his cock was as we talked over a drink for about an hour. He caressed my legs, and I was going wild as his fingers started probing into my wet pussy. I seriously had to fight the urge to accept Tony's offer to join him in his car so he could lick my cunt! God, how I wanted to ask him how big his prick was!

Yes, I wanted to suck and fuck them all, but I was getting smart enough to realize that I had to come up with a plan first. But the decision was made. I needed throngs of men with hot big cocks and loads of fresh cum. It would be soon, but for now, it would have to be another day.

It was time to go home.

Chapter 25

When I went back to work the next day, I stormed into Jack's office.

I still couldn't believe that he really thought of me as a whore, and that he pimped me to help his career. The fact that I had wonderful sex with Jamar and his driver didn't matter.

The infuriation never died down from the day before. Even my husband noticed. All I told him was that my boss was being a royal asshole. It was true. I just didn't tell Mark that he was an asshole pimp.

Jack told me to relax and have a seat. I did, but I was clearly angry. He stood in front of me, leaning against the front of his desk. He asked me how it went, and I just told him that Jamar said we could have his accounts.

Jack already knew. He told me that Jamar came to the bank just after fucking me. He said Jamar was quite pleased.

Jack walked up to me as he recounted the details of how the Arabs had fucked me. I was surprised Jamar had told him. But the details were getting me wet . . . again.

Jack stood before me and unzipped his pants. Apparently, he had forgotten my condition for going to bed with Jamar. Or he just didn't care. He knew I was a cock monster who couldn't say no when one was stuck in my face.

He pulled out his prick and pushed it toward my face. Like a woman taking a drink of water, I nonchalantly slipped the cock head into my mouth as he told me more of the details. I pushed the thin prick deep into my mouth and throated it.

I was getting very wet hearing the details of how Jamar and his driver fucked my ass. I reached between my legs and started rubbing my clit. Yes, I thought. I could get angry later. Now, I just wanted to rub one off!

Jack put his hand on the back of my head and pulled me off from the chair. He made me get on my knees and tell him every detail from my perspective while I sucked his cock. What a pervert, I thought.

I sucked, stopped and talked, and then sucked again. I would deep throat his prick between every part of the story. It was really exciting him. I could taste the pre-cum oozing from his cock.

I was soon rewarded with a gush of sticky goo in my mouth. I just let it dribble out, licking it around my lips as he collapsed back in his chair.

That was it for Jack.

With the way Jamar made me feel, I realized I didn't need this asshole any more. I wanted to give him one last blowjob that he would never forget.

After I swallowed his load, I stood up and told him there would be no more whoring around and no more office flings with him.

Jack got up and tried to intimidate me, but it only made my resolve firmer. He got pissed and started to come over to me. I bolted for the door.

I looked at Jack as pissed as I've ever been, adding that his wife could sort this out if he didn't like it.

Jack just shook his head, probably figuring that I would calm down and change my mind. I wouldn't. I knew then and there that I was done with this asshole.

I probably would have calmed down, and I probably would have gone back to our sick relationship if it were any other man. The fact was, however, he was a total user. What's more, the louse had a small cock compared to a real stud, and he never could make me cum. Let's face it. I was risking everything by committing adultery. Why should I risk it on a loser like that?

No, Jamar and his driver made me realize a few things.

I was a slut and I enjoyed being used and abused in bed by men. I loved the taste and feel of a hard cock in my throat, and I got cock-crazed if I didn't get enough.

I also need HUGE cock. Very long and very thick. And I needed it deep up my cunt and ass, preferably at the same time! D.P. A unique sex act that convinced me that God wants women to be happy.

I also realized that I was a cum slut, a woman who had to taste man juice mixed with my lipstick.

Yes, I was a slut, a true blue slut. A size queen, an ass whore, a blowjob addict, a cum slut. No sense hiding the truth.

Two things were for certain.

I'd take any cock, but why settle for a small one when I was clearly a size queen? Why not seek out truly big cock?

I also had to be smart about satisfying my needs. If I didn't control how and when I got cock, I'd be a whore who would let any man use her. That didn't bode so well for me in the past, so I knew that I had to take the initiative.

The only problem would be dealing with my husband. I had to protect my marriage.

I worked on solving these problems that entire week. I came to the conclusion that I quickly needed to find a replacement stud until I could solve the other issues.

But who?

I thought about Bill, but he was a transient. While I'd surely fuck him again if I saw him, he just wasn't regular enough to solve a regular need.

I thought about Al, but the fucker was too risky. With all of those friends of his who knew me in a carnal sense, the risk of exposure was just too high.

That was a problem that I couldn't solve today. All I knew was that I needed to get LAID. I just didn't know who I could find to do it. I needed cock, any cock except for Jacks. Someone safe.

Hopefully someone with a big cock.

Chapter 26

For some reason, I felt myself being inexplicably drawn back to the Roundup. I knew it would be a good place to prowl for a hard cock.

The day I decided to go, I had on a silky-like, sleeveless dress that was low-cut with three buttons at the top. It went mid-way between my waist and my knees.

Because my dress was so short, I had to wear my crotchless pantyhose. The tops of the stockings would have shown. I picked tan ones for today.

Same jewelry, wedding ring, and makeup as usual. Red lipstick and nails, and black high heels. Perfume. I looked and smelled great, and I knew it.

At the end of work that day, I called my husband and told him that a friend at work was having problems with her husband. I was going shopping with her, but I may be home late if she wanted to talk. What a line!

I walked into the Roundup about 4:30 pm. It was a Friday night, so there were more people there than usual, and most of the men locked their eyes on me when I walked in. I loved it. I just strut in, my long legs showing for every man to see. I went to a bar stool and sat down.

I had to be careful. I was going to let some lucky bastard pick me up, but it had to be safe. I glanced around the room, and received a surprise I wasn't expecting. Of all the people to find, it was Bill!

I walked over to Bill with the resolve that he was going to stud me tonight. I knew this bastard who popped me the first time last year couldn't resist me.

I walked next to Bill and asked him how he was doing. He introduced me to his two trucker friends, Pete and Sam. Pete asked me if I wanted to join them. A triple fuck, I thought! I didn't hesitate to accept the offer.

Both men were about as old as Bill, and they were dressed the same way. Old pants, and a dirty white tee-shirt covering a pot belly. The truckers also had a lot of tattoos, but I didn't care. It certainly didn't stop us from striking up a good conversation!

The men complimented me on my outfit, and I made sure to cross and uncross my legs regularly to show them my legs at every opportunity.

As the evening wore on, I exposed more of my legs for the men to enjoy. But I made certain to make sure they couldn't see my panties to prevent them from making a show.

As we sat and drank, and I reveled in the attention being showered on me by these men. I laughed and joked with these horny old bastards like I was a barroom tramp. I realized the incredible high a woman can get by cock teasing men who desperately wanted to get laid!

I leaned over the table a few times to talk, their eyes popping from their heads as they saw my big tits hanging down. Bill ate it up, reaching over to rub my leg so his friends could see. I didn't stop him. In fact, I really though he'd try to feel up my tits!

I added to the whorish atmosphere by touching up my lipstick at the table, running my tongue over my lips as I finished. I also made my hair look more sluttish by running my hands wildly through it as we laughed. I had everyone in the room watching our table!

I knew my goal was being accomplished without much real effort. I was teasing the hell out of these trucker's cocks, making them wonder if I wanted to get screwed. Hard-ons were definitely developing at that table!

As we talked and drank some more, I was surprised when Bill started to bring his friends in on what he had done to me. He started by asking if I took his advice on stockings, to which I replied that I had.

Bill then asked if I was wearing stockings then, and I told him I wasn't. He said he was disappointed, so I told him I had to show him what I was wearing, because they were just as good.

I took Bill by the hand and led him to a recessed area by the bathrooms. I hiked my dress up in front to show him my crotchless pantyhose. When he saw me, he looked like a kid in a candy shop!

The lech wasted no time stuffing his hand beside my panties to cop a feel, pressing me against the wall and kissing me at the same time. I returned the kiss, as he slipped his fingers into my wet cunt.

"Fuck, Andrea," he said, "you're so fucking wet."

"You make me wet, Bill," I told him.

"You're gonna get fucked by me tonight," he said, "you know that, right?"

I didn't answer him. I just moaned as he continued fingering me.

Bill then brought his head around mine and started kissing my neck.

"God, I want you baby," he whispered, "let's go back to my truck again and fuck."

"Wait, Bill" I said, "the evening is young. I promise I'll sleep with you!"

I was still disgusted at what the fucker had done to me last year. Yes, I eventually loved it. But he did it in such a brutal way that pissed me off. Now it was my turn. Why should he enjoy me all alone? Was he the kind of guy who could share his prize with his friends, or would it drive him insanely jealous? We were about to see.

I took Bill by the hand and led him back to the table. I squeezed his hand as we walked, clearly indicating that I was serious. I would fuck him tonight.

Bill's friends were wondering what the hell was going on, and their silent questioning intensified when Bill openly started rubbing his hand far up my dress to reveal my panties and crotchless pantyhose.

I let the letch do as he will, seeing just how horny his friends would become. Their speculation was soon confirmed when Bill surprisingly started to brag about how he ruined me for my husband.

"I met this young lady about a year ago," he told his friends. "She was a sad, lonely housewife who didn't know what she was missing by getting some cock on the side," he added.

I smiled as he told the story.

"I sure took care of that problem, didn't I sweetheart?" he grimaced.

I smiled and reached over to give him a deep kiss in front of his friends.

"Yep," he went on as he felt me up, "I humped the ever loving shit out of her right in my rig!"

The three old leches laughed out loud, obviously entranced with the thought that they, too, would love to hump me.

"Is that right, Andrea?" Sam asked with a wide grin.

Ok, why not. I'll praise Bill in front of his friends. I wanted to excite my first stud so he would be inclined to truly service me tonight.

"Bill has such a big cock, Sam," I said.

I think the men were stunned that I admitted it, and that I talked to them that way. Their eyes widened and their smiles grew as I went on.

"I have to admit it," I said, "Bill really knows how to screw a woman senseless!"

Bill smiled and leaned over to kiss me. I kissed him back in front of his friends, being sure to let them see me work my tongue into his mouth.

Bill stopped kissing me to add a very true comment.

"You boys ain't had a piece until you've had a classy lady like this! Her pussy is just as tight as a virgin!"

I should have been offended, but I was starting to get drunk and I just didn't care. Besides, I knew he was right. Those old bastards haven't had a piece unless they met someone like me.

Bill then reached over and planted another wet kiss on my lips as he took a feel of my tits. I hungrily returned the kiss.

Sam then spoke up to break the kiss.

"So, how 'bout letting us judge for ourselves!" he said in a question that was more of a statement.

I looked at Sam and asked a question I knew the answer to. It was a question Sam wanted to hear.

"You want me to do all three of you?" I asked with an innocent tone.

He was quick to reply.

"What's wrong, Andrea, can't you handle three men at once?"

The dare was thrown out.

Bill didn't like the idea of sharing his catch. Before I could accept the challenge, Bill interjected.

"I don't know," he said.

He paused for a moment and then came up with an excuse.

"It was awful hard opening her up," he added, "I wouldn't want to see her hurt."

Pete and Sam started to shake their heads in disbelief. Bill went on with his excuse.

"Besides, she's married," like that made any difference to him or anyone else.

Bill didn't know about the scores of men since him. He didn't know how much of a fuck queen I'd become since he first ruined me. I didn't think these old fuckers could hurt me if they wanted to.

My plan was coming together well. Bill was uncomfortable at the idea of sharing me. The rat bastard deserved to be uncomfortable after the way he practically raped me last year. Yes, let the fucker watch his friends enjoy using me to service their cocks, I thought.

Without even looking at Bill, I leaned over the table in front of Sam's scruffy face.

"You wanna screw me Sam?" I asked, "you want me to screw all three of you? I can handle the three of you in my sleep!"

Sam immediately snatched up my acceptance. He took me by the hand and we stood up. He wrapped his arms around me, his hand on my ass.

"There's a motel a few miles from her, he said, "let's go there."

We turned and started to walk out. Sam was pulling me along by the hand. Bill and Pete followed closely behind. The truckers found a nice piece of ass!

The men all had 18-wheelers, so I ended up driving them. We took my soccer mom minivan. Bill sat in front, and Sam and Pete got in back. Bill hiked my dress and rubbed my pussy as I drove. Sam saw this, so reached in front and rubbed my tits through my dress. God, it felt to damn good!

When we got to the seedy strip motel, the three men threw some cash together and Pete got the room. It was a dive room, obviously made for truckers who didn't like their little sleepers. Or a place they brought their truck stop whores. It didn't matter that much, I thought. It served the purpose.

As the hotel door slammed shut, I knew my fate for the night was sealed.

Chapter 27

Sam wasted no time in his effort to test Bill's statement. He grabbed me from behind and ground his hard-on into my ass as soon as the door was shut.

Kissing my neck, the letch used one hand to squeeze my tits and another to feel up my cunt through my silky dress, forcefully pulling my ass into his hard-on as he did so. I leaned my head back to return his hot kiss, reaching back down between his legs for his stiff cock.

As Bill watched, he started with his commentary.

"I told you she was a horny cunt," he boasted to his friends.

"That's fine with me," Sam shot back as he continued fondling me.

As Sam continued kissing me, he reached under my dress and ran his hand behind my legs. My panties were dripping wet.

"Fuck," he said, "this bitch is WET!"

"Good," said Bill, "'cause she's got three hard cocks to take care of with that tight cunt of hers!"

The guys stripped as Sam continued feeling me up, stroking his hands up and down my legs and squeezing my bush. Bill and Pete were down to nothing but their tee-shirts in an instant.

Pete then broke us up.

"Hey, wait a minute," he said, "how 'bout sharing her with us!"

Sam turned to tell him to fuck off, pushing my face into the wall and unzipping his pants to let his stiff prick out. Damn, now they were fighting over me like a pack of hungry dogs!?!

Pinned with my face against the wall, Sam hiked my dress up from behind and literally ripped off my flimsy panties. Seeing my crotchless fishnet pantyhose again, he was quick to add his own thoughts.

"This cunt came ready for hard cock," he said gleefully.

His statement made me moan, and I spread my legs a little bit to accommodate the fuck stick that was sure to be jammed into me. To add to the whorish show, I reached back and slipped my long fingernails into my slit to open my pussy for him.

That's not what Sam was thinking!

"Fuck your cunt lips, bitch, my horny pecker wants a piece of that nice ass as promised!" he retorted.

Sam pinned me to the wall with his hands on my ass cheeks, and pried them apart for his prick. I didn't fight him. I wanted it.

Sam's cock head felt huge and hot as it probed for my pink hole. Before I knew it, the bastard had the head of his old cock stuck in my ass. The fucker had easily opened my ass to have his way with me.

I lifted my arms and braced myself against the wall for the brutal ass fucking that was sure to come, my wedding rings glistening from the bright overhead light.

"Agggggh . . . ," I cried out, my ass betraying me by tightening in only s few days.

I could feel my legs start to buckle from the force of the cock penetration, and I squirmed my ass to settle on the huge invader.

"Agggggh . . . ," I cried out again.

Sam was merciless.

"Squirm and moan all you want, bitch, 'cause I'm not stopping 'til my cock's deep in your tight ass!" he gloated.

The bastard pushed harder, his huge cock boring into my asshole. His cock was not as big as Jamar's, but it was still pretty big. I squirmed and let out a whimper from the feel of my ass being so harshly taken.

"Go ahead and whimper, you fucking cunt, 'cause you're taking all of my cock if I have to rip your pretty tight ass open!" he said in a cold manner.

I braced my legs as I stood pinned against the wall. Both of us were moaning as the cock head slowly inched deeper and deeper inside of me. I swear I could feel every inch of Sam's hard cock as it buried itself into my ass.

Sam then reach around me to the top of my dress as he pushed his cock. I felt his hands grab a side of my dress and pull. I could hear the buttons flying as he ripped the top open. Goddamn! This horny fucker was just taking what he wanted!

Once he had my dress open, Sam stopped pushing his cock for a moment. The cock was about halfway inside of me, the hot prick just throbbing in my ass as he kept it there. Sam then reached into my dress and pulled my bra down with his hands.

I could feel the cool air sweep across me as my aching tits popped out of my bra. Sam grabbed one with each hand and squeezed the nipples hard as he started pushing his cock back into me. Oh God! It felt so good to have the hard cock using my ass, and those rough hands enjoying my firm tits!

"I've wanted to feel up these tits all night!" he said.

Excited by the spectacle of my being pinned against the wall by an old man driving a huge cock into my ass as he kneaded my tits was too much for Bill and Sam. They started making lewd comments.

"Oh fuck!" Pete said hungrily, "look at those magnificent tits!"

"That whole fucking body is hot," Bill replied.

"Damn! Sam sure is giving it to her," Pete said.

Bill replied by boasting of his prior conquest of my ass.

"Bitch screamed her head off when I popped her virgin ass for the first time, but she was slamming her ass on my cock in no time."

A true statement, I thought as Sam probed my ass deeper.

I thought Sam had a few inches to go when suddenly the mammoth cock bolted the rest of the way up my ass. I was imbedded me up to his heavy balls and could feel the fuck stick throb in my ass.

"Uggghhhh . . . God," I blurted out from the unforeseen ruthless act.

"Ah . . . fuck, yeah" Sam responded with pride.

When Sam started to withdraw his cock, I let out a deep, long groan and my legs started to tremble more. Having experienced my first searing orgasm of the evening when Sam bore into me, I pushed my ass out in submission so he could give me a real ass fucking.

I reached down between my legs and started rubbing my clit. My pussy was so wet, I couldn't believe it. I just rubbed and rubbed, reach back and touching his balls with my fingernails when Sam stroked into me.

Sam then started telling me what he wanted as he started to pile drive me.

"Lick your lips now that you have my hard prick up your ass, you fucking tease, you ass whore," he commanded.

I kicked my head back on my shoulder, and glanced back at him at him as I licked my lips. I moaned loudly, enticing the bastard to butt fuck my loosening hole by acknowledging my new nickname.

"Fuck my ass. Yes. Yes. I'm an ass whore, and I need my ass fucked hard," I cried out.

Sam obliged with the lusty submission, causing his massive balls to viciously slap against my ass cheeks. The feeling was overwhelming. My head swooned and my hair began to thrash around as Sam literally sodomized me.

Pete offered yet another comment as I took Sam's cock up my ass.

"This ass slut sure looks good with a hard cock up her ass," he said.

"Look at her rubbing herself while Sam gives it to her!"

Always ready to respond to a crude remark, Bill predicted the fun to come.

"Wait 'till the bitch starts sucking cock," he said, "she can suck a golf ball through a garden hose!"

"God damn!" Pete responded as he stroked his cock harder. He then walked up to me and Sam and put his hand out. He reached between my legs and coped a feel of my pussy.

"Fuck, she's wet!" he told his friends.

It turned Sam on even more. He beat my ass with his large cock, groaning out at least three times with my new name.

"Ahhhh . . .Take my hard pecker in your ass, Andrea ass whore."

I felt the large cock head split my ass open each time it banged home. It felt so good, I was going crazy. I leaned over to kiss Pete, and he was quick to oblige.

As Sam was really putting it to me, I looked over to see Bill stroking his erection and waiting for his turn.

"Really give it to me boys," I moaned over to them.

"I want to get fucked so bad tonight!"

Bill responded quickly.

"We'll give it to you baby, you wait and see!"

Pete slipped his fingers up my cunt as he offered me some advice. It caused me to start moaning uncontrollably.

"Take all his cock, slut, 'cause you're taking mine in the ass next," he said.

Sam pounded my ass like a madman for about ten minutes. He then stiffened his back and popped his load deep into my guts.

The old stud wretched his cock out of me in a flash, and then literally threw me onto the floor so his friends could take me next.

I wasn't without hard cock for but an instant. I laid there on my side, and lifted myself up by my elbows. I looked up at Pete and Bill, and I saw their long horny dongs waving at me. God, seeing these old truckers with those gorgeous big cocks!

Maybe I shouldn't have been such a cock tease. Nah! I did the right thing!

I had incredible luck, I thought, to land so many well hung studs, old as they were. Hungry for the huge cocks I saw in front of me, I crawled over to the two men on my hands and knees like a whore in heat. I opened my mouth, waiting for horny cock.

I leaned up and let them push their cocks into my mouth together. Here was a first, if you can believe it. I don't remember ever having two cocks in my mouth at the same time!

I reached out and took their two cocks in my hands, jacking them until they were good and stiff. I sucked Pete into my mouth, while continuing to jack Bill's cock, my hot mouth causing him to moan.

I immediately started to alternatively deep throat both Bill and Pete, jacking the other while I had one lodged in my throat.

"I see I taught you good, you cock sucking cunt," Bill spat out.

I withdrew his throbbing organ long enough to look Bill in the eye to respond.

"You really taught me to suck hard cock baby," I said to the victor.

He smiled as I continued.

"God I love your big hot prick, Bill."

Sam, sitting on the bed, heard my comment.

"God damn," Sam said, "what a fucking whore you created Bill."

I stopped to look him in the eye and moan my approval.

"Ummmm . . ." I moaned, "Bill turned me into a cum slut too!"

Pete responded with a lewd comment as Bill started laughing, his prick now in my mouth.

"Damn, should we shoot wads on her face, or pump 'em up her cunt?" he asked his friends.

"I don't care guys," I said, "I just need to feel your hot cum!"

I continued sucking Bill and Pete, reaching between their legs to rub their assholes during their suck job. They moaned as I rubbed my soft finger over their old assholes, and it apparently turned Sam on again.

Stripping down to only his tee-shirt, he went and washed his dirty pecker off in the sleazy bathroom. The filthy bastard then came back for more of me, not waiting for his friends to finish their turns. He was ready for his second piece of my hot ass.

The old stud came up behind me and kneeled down. Knowing I was about to be fucked, I again reached back between my legs to open my hairy slit with my long fingernails as Sam hiked up my dress.

The bastard saw what I was doing, and he loved it.

"Yeah, baby, spread those pretty cunt lips for my hot prick, you fucking slut."

Sam then grabbed my waist with one hand, and savagely bulldozed his big cock into my cunt with the other. My cunt tightly sheathed the hard prick that was so swiftly jammed into it.

Gripping my waist with such force that I still had hand marks later that night, Sam fucked me like a horny old fucker who hadn't had a piece in months. You wouldn't have known that he just gotten off in my ass.

I was going crazy. I loved being fucked, and I didn't hesitate to tell him. I stopped sucking cock for a moment.

"God Sam," I moaned, "you're such a big-cocked fucking stud!"

"I'm just getting started," he bragged.

Excited by the show, Bill took me by the head and brutally mouth fucked me. It was no time before I could feel his hot seed shooting all over my face.

"Ahhhh . . . ," he groaned, "here's a load for your pretty face!"

The fucker shot another magnificent load, just as he had in the cab of his truck a year ago. God, how I missed the cum of his man who trained me!

I wanted to inflame the pack of horny bastards more, so I licked the cum that was on my lips. The rest of the cum made a complete mess, gravity causing some to drips down my chin and onto my perky tits.

I immediately began to collect the sticky wad drippings on my tits and chin with my fingers. I rubbed the globs of cum all around my face as Sam continued banging himself off in my cunt. I mixed the hot cum with my lipstick, pulling the globs to my tongue. Long webs of cum were constantly running from my face to my fingers.

Sam loved it. He reached out and tweaked my nipples as he pumped my cunt. The cum on my tits greased them for him. The feelings of cum and brutal treatment made my nipples grow an inch!

I then took Bill's softening prick into my mouth, sucking hard to make sure I had his balls thoroughly cleaned out. After I finished, I looked down at the wet cum stain that was deposited on my dress.

Sam just rammed me deeper and deeper as I enjoyed what he was doing to my tits, the thrill of Bill's hot seed causing me to buck my cunt wildly into the fucker behind me.

Pete was more of a stallion, and a mean fucker, too. Pete wanted a piece of my ass, and he wanted it now.

"Well, Sam, was her ass as good as Bill told us it would be?" Pete asked.

Sam, wildly stroking my cunt, grunted a response.

"I'll fuck this bitch all night!" Sam moaned.

Pete demanded that he be let in, and Sam told him to wait a minute. What a sight it was to see these three old men fighting over my holes!

Sam withdrew from my cunt, but only for a second. He laid flat on the floor, and pulled me on top of him. Knowing what he was planning, I crawled on top of him and impaled my cunt deep on his thick cock.

I bent down towards Sam and started french kissing him as we fucked. He kissed me back passionately as I pushed my ass straight in the air. I gave an open invitation for Pete to double penetrate me.

Pete was ready. As he walked up to me, he commented on what he saw.

"Bitch's ass is still gaped," he said, my asshole still wide open from the massive ass pounding Sam gave me with that coke-bottle thick cock of his.

My experiences that month taught me that begging for mercy turns men on. I looked over to Pete as he started to walk up to my ass with his huge dong waiving.

"Oh God, you bastards aren't both going to fuck me?" I asked.

Pete felt like a man in control, intent on giving me that double penetration I desperately needed.

"Fucking right, cunt," he growled, "go tell your husband we double fucked you like a whore."

Straddling Sam's legs, Pete took his enormous prick and started to mount my ass. He split my crack with his rough hands and positioned his cock. As he skewered me by pushing the throbbing mushroom cock head into my gaping asshole, he calmly and coolly told me what he thought.

"Now let's see about how good this ass really is," he said as he mounted me.

I begged in response with enticing lies.

"Oh God, I can't take both of your big cocks! Please, no!"

As I expected, Pete had no compassion.

"Fuck you, you fucking horny slut, you need a good, hard double fucking!"

Pete grunted as he pushed the cock head into my ass, causing me to groan from the delightful feeling of having two cocks in me at the same time.

I enticed the bastards further.

"Oh God, you horny bastards," I cried, "you're splitting me apart with those giant cocks!"

Ramming his cock into my ass harder, Pete retorted with a grunt.

"That's what you get for teasing us all night, you fucking cock tease, hard peckers stuffed up both your cunt and your ass!"

I moaned like a whore in heat hearing those truthful words.

Pete was soon in to my ass up to his balls, leaning down to ask me a vile question.

"How does two hard cocks feel, you fucking bitch?"

I turned my head to him, and gave him a wet kiss, driving my tongue deep into his troat. I stopped to grunt a response.

"I love your hard cocks . . ."

Pete then pulled away from me, and I yelled to my fuckers.

"I am a tease. Punish me with your hard cocks!"

"Fucking right, you hot cunt," Pete yelled out.

The trucker stud started to long dick my ass while Sam worked my cunt from the bottom.

I was now full of hard cock. Truly full of rock hard, throbbing cock. My stuffed body was aflame with pure lust. I started moaning uncontrollably.

I started to cry for a good banging. The old leches delivered. The double fucking was heaven as the old men really gave it to me.

"Oh God," I cried, "so much cock!"

"God, your cocks are so fucking big!"

"Enjoy it baby," Bill responded cooly as he enjoyed the show.

"They're so fucking hard . . . Ohhhh God," I moaned.

Sam bucked his waist to poke his rod in and out as best he could. The guy on the bottom always seems to get a little less of the action because of the position. Oh well, I thought, that was Sam's problem.

"Oh fuck she feels good," Pete said.

I moaned in response, knowing how great his cock felt in me.

Pete reared back and repeatedly steamrolled my ass as I moaned. The smell of sex was thick in the air. It was all so decadent.

"Yeah, baby, take these cocks you ass whore," he gloated as he long stroked me.

I relished the feeling of these two cocks. I was happily taking it all.

"You've created a real whore here, Bill," Sam said as he squeezed my tits.

"Damn right," Bill replied, "popped the bitch in my truck last year. Had only been with her husband before that day."

"Bullshit!" Sam yelled back.

"She was fucking with you Bill," he said as he pushed, "this bitch had to have been a cock whore since high school!"

I was moaning uncontrollably the whole time. His words brought a deep groan from me. My swooning head was thrashing around uncontrollably, my hair flying around everywhere as I thoroughly enjoyed the brutal fucking I was getting.

Pete responded to my moans.

"Fucking whore needs more cock, Bill."

I moaned again in agreement.

Bill, too, agreed. "Yeah, guess she needs a hard cock down her throat too!"

The scene was incredibly hot, and it made Bill hard again in no time. The dirty bastard walked up to me with his hard pecker poised for my mouth.

"Open up, baby," he commanded.

I opened my mouth and Bill slipped the cock in. I gobbled it up as Pete slammed into my asshole harder, Sam stroking me from below.

"Yep," Bill responded, "time to feed this married bitch more hard cock."

Bill pulled back hard, dragging his cock out of my mouth despite the great suction I had on it. He waved his long prick in my face, knowing that I would keep trying to snap it up.

I kept pushing myself forward to get it into my mouth, but the fucker kept pulling back teasing me. Every so often he would rub the cock on my lips, and then pull it away as I tried to suck it in.

I finally couldn't wait any more. I reached up with my hand and grabbed the massive tool. I pulled Bill close to me and took the shaft into my mouth.

"Damn this girl's hungry for cock!" Bill said.

With that, he proceeded to mouth fuck me, just as he did in the cab of his truck last year. He was brutal, holding my head with his two hands and slamming his prick in and out of my throat.

As Bill used my mouth like a pussy, I groaned from the intense action. I loved it! Now I was truly full of cock! And I didn't want it to stop!

I moaned and moaned, ecstatic to be full of so much fiery hot cock so skillfully handled by ruthless old studs. My body was literally spasming. Here I was, thoroughly impaled by large horny cocks, cumming uncontrollably and deeply moaning the whole time.

The triple fucking went on for a good twenty minutes. Cock rolled into my mouth, cunt and ass, each man sharing more and more thoughts about their "ass whore." I loved it. I wanted to feel and hear more.

I was floating on a tremendous high from the intense feeling of it all when suddenly Pete withdrew from my ass as blew a load on my hiked dress.

"Wear my cum, ass whore, so everyone can see what a horny bitch you are," Pete said.

Sam wasn't far behind, spunking up my slick vaginal canal. I could feel his hot cum oozing out of my cunt and onto his balls.

After my studs had used me, I crawled off from Sam and kneeled in front of Bill. I was still mesmerized by this huge prick that seduced me last year and broke me in to this wanton, lascivious lifestyle. I wanted to suck that beautiful prick some more.

I decided to give Bill's magnificent cock the deep throating it so richly deserved. I reached back and started rubbing my clit as I mouth-fucked him. Just like my master taught me last year!

"God damn, fuck whore can sure throat a cock," Pete said from a distance.

I pulled my head off from Bill's throbbing cock for a short moment.

"I love a huge prick in my throat," I teased them. "A big, thick, hard COCK!"

Bill didn't need the talk. He just grabbed my head and started slamming his cock into my throat over and over. Each time he forced it in up to his balls.

"Damn!" Pete said, "this bitch should do a *Throat Gaggers* video!"

I moaned again, feeling like a true porn star. It made me want to do more. So I forced my tongue out and licked Bill's balls while his shaft was imbedded in my throat. I serviced Bill like this repeatedly for a few minutes. The letch was in heaven.

"Ahhhh . . .," he said, "suck my cock you fucking whore."

"Damn!" Pete said, "I wish I had a video camera!"

The old bastard then leaned back on the floor, his beer belly sticking out and his legs spread wide. His massive log stood stiff, ready to be serviced some more. Now free from my other fuckers, I got on my knees and crawled between his legs.

I took the rod in my hand and gripped it tightly. I started to jack it up and down while I looked Bill in the eye, licking my lips as I gave him a hand job. He reached down and stroked my hair and tits. He grabbed my nipples and pulled on them as hard as he could, making me groan.

I popped the large prick in my mouth as I jerked the shaft and sucked as hard as I could as Bill worked over my tits. I then pulled the hot dick out, allowing drool to run all the way down from my lips to his massive cock head.

I was creating a show for Bill and his friends that they would never forget! As I sucked, I kept looking around at the men. I wanted to show them what they had.

I sucked on Bill's stiff pole with reckless abandon, occasionally jacking the big cock and reaching down to lick his big balls, quite a show for Sam and Pete. During the course of the blowjob, Bill looked down at me and asked loudly.

"Hey, did I ever knock you up?"

He remembered, I thought. I knew this comment would entice the other fuckers.

I wanted to arose the dirty bastards more, so I just moaned and nodded yes with his big bone lodged in my throat.

Pete saw my answer, and yelled back to Bill.

"You knocked this married ass whore up? Damn!"

Bill gave a smirk little response.

"She begged me to soak her eggs in seed!"

Sam looked down at me and sought confirmation.

"That right, you ass whore, you want men to implant you, you married cunt?"

Again, I nodded yes with my throat impaled on Bill's cock, moaning louder to let them know just how much I had wanted it.

"I love getting knocked up by studs with big cocks," I said.

I knew that line shook the men and excited them more.

I thought I would try it again. I abruptly stopped the suck job, and looked up at Bill. I knew he would love it if I acknowledged him to his friends as a man who really took me.

"Bill, would you please fuck me? I need to feel your big prick creaming between my legs."

Bill loved it!

"Fucking cunt loves my cock," he said, looking back at his friends.

I laid flat on my back and hiked up my dress. Remembering how wonderful it felt when he first laid me, I eagerly spread my legs wide so he could lay me again. I looked up at Bill as I dug my heels into the floor, bracing myself for him to take me.

Bill rolled over and climbed between my legs, stroking his cock to get it prepared to mount me. The stud moaned a happy acknowledgment as he slipped his big cock head into me again.

As Bill pushed his cock into my slicked up hole, I savored the feel of every inch of his bone jammed up between my legs. It brought back all of the memories of that first evening a year ago. God, how he changed me in one short instant!

We then started to kiss.

Bill slow stroked me for a few minutes while we lovingly french kissed. He then lifted my legs high around my neck. He proceeded to long dick in front of his friends, and I made sure I moaned the whole time.

"Yes, Yes, fuck me, fuck me hard lover," I screamed.

"Oh God Bill, you turned me into a fucking whore, and now I can't live without your big thick cock stroking between my legs!"

Bill responded in like fashion.

"Here's your cock, you fucking horny sweet little bitch," he grunted.

"Your loser husband can't, but I'll service that married cunt of yours!"

That hurt my feelings, but unfortunately it was true. But I didn't want to lose the moment. So I continued.

"God, yes, Bill, splash my ripe eggs with your fucking seed like Sam just did . . . knock my married cunt up again!"

Bill was quick to give his reply.

"I'll knock you up every time you see me, you fucking tramp!"

With those statements out, it was only a matter of time before he blew again. Sure enough, the talk of impregnating a woman had the same effect it always does. Bill started to slam his cock deep into me harder. He tensed up and started screaming.

"Fucking cunt . . . married . . . fucking hot cunt."

I loved it when I felt his hot prick creaming deep between my legs once again.

Bill collapsed onto me, his head next to mine. I turned and whispered in his ear.

"I've missed you so much, Bill."

He kissed me gently.

"I missed you too sweetheart."

It was too much for Pete. He was the only one who hadn't cum twice, and he was jerking off the whole time he watched Bill screw me. The old trucker stud came up to me and Bill.

"This fucking cunt, . . . I'll give this fucking cunt some hot seed!" Pete said.

"Get off her you fucker," he screamed at Bill.

Bill slowly dismounted me and rolled over on his side to watch the action. He was quickly replaced with Pete.

Pete spread my legs with his while he held himself up by his elbows. He didn't need to hold his cock to find the mark. It bobbed around for a second, and then I felt it slip into me. I was so wet by now, it had no problem gliding right into me.

Pete started to furiously jerk his cock off in my cunt. I enticed him more.

"God, your cock feels so good stroking off between my legs!"

Pete humped me harder as he heard my words. It also inflamed the others. As Pete took me, I reached over and grabbed Bill's stiffening prick. In a flash I was also straddled by Sam, his cock dangling in front of me.

Pete wanted to make sure he gave me a good creaming, so he pinned my legs up with his strong arms. He slammed into me deeper and deeper with long, forceful strokes.

Sam couldn't take it. He had his fuck stick throbbing again in no time. He squatted down so he could feed it to me. Before I knew it, Pete was cumming again.

"Damn bitch!" he moaned, "you damn dirty little bitch!"

I'm sure he didn't have much cum left in those old balls, but I was happy to take whatever I could get. The same was true for Sam.

As Pete collapsed, I looked up at Sam to inflame the bastard.

"Cream in me too, Sam!" I cried.

Sam pulled Pete off from me and climbed between my legs. My slick cunt accepted his tool quite easily.

"Fuck me, you stud," I enticed him.

"Knock me up with that big cock of yours!"

"Fucking bitch," Sam grunted back as he pumped furiously.

The other men were focused on the fuck show. It even caused Pete to exclaim loudly.

"Christ, Bill, you created quite a fucking slut."

"That's one beautiful pussy," Bill responded.

I bucked back at Sam's forceful fucking, intent on drawing the seed from his balls. I licked his ear and enticed him the whole time.

"Go ahead, you fucking horny stud, cum in me!"

It wasn't too much longer before Sam tensed up. He lifted my legs even further and slammed the fuck tool into me one last time. I could feel his balls twitch as they emptied the sperm into me.

Sam dismounted me quickly, being sure to shake the last thick strings of his cum onto the front of my dress. As soon as he was up, I leaned up on my elbows.

Looking at Pete and Bill, I licked my lips.

"Any more fellas," I asked.

"I told you I could fuck you 'till you drop!"

I could see the wheels spinning in their perverted minds from my statement, which I knew they took as an offer.

As Pete moved back to the bed to recuperate, Sam and Bill just looked at me lying on the floor, thinking what they should do with me next.

I asked the men if the piece of ass was as advertised, and they all acknowledged with various profanities that it was.

"Fucking right, you bastards," I said as I started to get up.

"You horny old bastards will always remember Andrea's piece of hot married ass!"

As soon as I said that, I jumped up, grabbed my purse, and bolted for the door as my dress fell down. I had my fill for that night, so why stick around I figured!

The old studs jumped up to stop me, but I was outside before they could make it to the door. The sorry old bastards were naked and didn't want to be embarrassed! I kind of felt sorry for them. Here they were, horny and alone with each other. Oh well, it was their problem this time, not mine.

I thought about the night as I drove home. For three old truckers, they really were lucky to get a chance to fuck a woman like me! A young, beautiful wife who let them double fuck her like a whore. They got to do anything to me that they wanted, and any way they wanted to do it. I even deep throated them. I didn't owe them anything.

But there was still a problem.

The man that I loved.

Mark.

Chapter 28

I immediately got in my car and drove home, my mission fully accomplished.

The whole trip home I reveled in my conquest of Bill, seeing his eyes when I offered my ass to his two trucker friends! It was an incredible feeling.

Yes, I was a proud slut that night. I just let the three old bastards just take me any way they pleased! I felt deliciously satisfied by the intense three-man fuck job, and I wanted more!

I realized from this episode that I needed sex. I was voracious. The last year without strange cock was the hardest time in my life. And after this re-awakening, I knew I could never be denied more cock and cum. I found myself even considering Jamar's offer.

But I was confused and frustrated. I loved my husband so much, and I didn't want to live a sordid life of deceit and cheating. And I didn't want to hurt my family.

What was I to do? How could I even think of leaving my husband and my family? But what would I say if my daughters found out I was a rampant slut?

By the time I got home, I started to realize that cum residual had to be stuck somewhere. And my dress. Sam ripped off the buttons. Did it show?

I had to be careful. I tried to check the mirror when I got into the driveway, but it was just too dark. And even if I found cum or a tear in my dress, what could I do? I had to risk running into my husband when entered the house.

I walked into the house quietly, hoping to avoid Mark. I opened the door and tip-toed in. Shit! He was walking to meet me as I came in.

Mark looked at me, and I almost died. Cum was on me, he saw it. My dress. It was torn. Bruises. He saw bruises on me. I was paranoid.

My husband took me in his arms and kissed me. I panicked again. I thought for sure that he'd taste another man's cum in my mouth. I was surprised when he didn't.

It was then that I remembered that one of the men left a puddle of cum on the front of my dress that stained the material. Why hadn't Mark seen it yet?

When my husband finished kissing me, I quickly turned away from him and went up stairs to change.

Mark followed me, telling me how nice I looked.

Oh, damn! He's horny, I thought.

I've had at least six loads of cum. If he doesn't see or smell it, he'll see my opened fucked holes and know I've fucked around on him. How could I explain cum dripping from my cunt? My gaped asshole? Cum dripping from my cunt? And bruises. My poor abused tits had to be bruised!

As I went into the bathroom and shut the door, I told Mark I had a terrible night and just wasn't up for sex.

It was a lie.

I wanted so bad to fuck him, to taste my husband's cum. I was so afraid though, I just couldn't risk it Thankfully, Mark accepted it and went back downstairs.

I felt terrible, satisfying my needs and not his.

I went to the bathroom to take a shower and get into my pajamas. I was thinking the whole time.

Deep down, I knew that somehow we could both have all of our needs met, but I didn't know how to make it a reality. I just didn't know how to tell him. I needed cock, but I needed him too.

There was also the issue of him trying to enjoy what so many other men had already enjoyed. Mark was starting to get horny, and I knew I couldn't keep him off much longer. Besides, if I knew that bastard Jack, he'd be trying to blackmail me into sex by threatening to tell Mark.

I had to find a long-term solution to my problem NOW.

I figured the best thing to do was to let Mark fuck me. It had been about two months since he fucked me last, and I couldn't put him off much longer. I'd just make sure he didn't get a look at my gaped ass. And I'd douche to get some of the thick loads of cum out of my cunt. My mind kept racing. But he must expect me to be tight!?! What could I do about that? Nothing. Nothing at all.

Goddamn, I was so paranoid I was starting to freak out! There wasn't much I could do. I was trapped. It was time to just let Mark see how sloppy my holes had become. I'd tell him that I was seduced, and that I was turned into an uncontrollable slut. What else could I do? Besides, I was still horny!

I prayed that my loving husband would understand as I walked downstairs to take him to bed. I was so afraid. My God, how do I tell him?

Mark was sitting in an easy chair as I came up to him. I bent over and gave him a kiss, reaching down to rub his crotch.

"I thought you weren't feeling well," he said.

"I took a shower and I feel better," I said.

I then sat on his lap and put my arms around him.

"Mark, I love you and I want you to be happy," I said.

I then did something I had never done to him before. I got off from him and kneeled down between his legs. I unzipped his zipper.

Mark was pleasantly surprised to see me acting this way. He leaned his head back in the chair as I pulled out his stiffening cock.

I sucked on the cock head and licked the shaft, carefully rubbing his balls with my nails. He was like all the others, soon moaning his approval.

I bobbed my head on his cock for a few minutes, sucking hard on his stiff prick. I then took the throbbing stick and worked it slowly down my throat. Mark was surprised by my skill, reaching down to stroke my hair.

I finally got him all the way in and withdrew. I then took him into my throat again.

Mark looked down at me and started to ask, "Andrea, . . ."

He cut himself off.

"Never mind," he said softly, leaning his head back to enjoy the deep throat experience.

I knew that it would no time before I was swallowing a tremendous load of cum. Should I let it splash me, or should I silently swallow it? I didn't want him to see that I was suddenly a whore, and I was confused about what I should do. Paranoid again.

I looked up at Mark, and I asked him a question as I stroked his throbbing cock.

"Mark, if you could cum wherever you wanted, where would it be?"

I was surprised when he looked at me and smiled.

"Really?" he asked.

"Anywhere?"

"Anywhere, love," I responded with a smile.

"On your face," he said.

"You have a beautiful face, and I've always dreamed of cumming all over it!"

I was shocked. I guess Mark truly was a normal man, a man who got off seeing a woman spunked with cum.

The decision was made. I was ready to accommodate his wish. I looked at my husband and sincerely whispered to him, "I love you."

I then took the cock deep into my throat and tried to swallow with the pole stuck in me. The sensation was too much for him, and his cock jerked.

I quickly pulled the cock out and aimed it at my face as I looked at him.

"Cum on my face baby," I said, "right on my lips!"

I jerked Marks' cock as I told him what I wanted, and a huge glob of cum came flying out to crash on my closed mouth. It was quickly followed by another on my nose, and a third on my forehead.

I jerked the cock some more as I opened my mouth to swill the cum on my lips. I popped the cock back into my mouth and sucked the last cum from it.

Oh my God! Would he see that I was a cum slut? But I couldn't stop. I swilled his cum around inside my mouth with my tongue. I would make it his decision. Yes, that was the answer!

I opened my mouth, the cum obviously filling it. I looked at Mark and asked him.

"Do you want your wife to eat your cum, or spit?" I asked.

"Damn, Andrea," he said, "you can spit if you want to . . . but I'd love to see you swallow!"

Ok, I thought. He wants a cum show. I started rub the cum all around my face, long strings creating webs of cum between my fingers.

"Oh, God . . . Andrea," he said in obvious delight.

I took my fingers and collected the rest of the hot cum on my face. I drew it to my lips and again savored the taste.

Mark was coming down from his high as he watched me, moaning as he watched the decadent display.

I licked up all of the cum and swallowed, making sure he could see my throat move as the cum went down. I then got up and moved sat on his lap.

I kissed him.

"Do you taste your cum on my lips?" I asked.

"Oh fuck!" he moaned back, french kissing me deeply.

When we stopped kissing, I hugged him. I whispered in his ear as I ran my tongue around it.

"Did I please you sweetheart?" I asked.

He was quick to reply, "Oh, God, yes."

Mark then took me by the hand and led me upstairs to the bedroom. The moment of truth had arrived. He would surely know now.

When Mark took me in his arms and kissed me, I remembered all of the things

I learned about what men want. I stopped him, whispering in his ear that I wanted to freshen up for him.

"But you just showered," he responded.

"I want to really give you a night to remember," I said.

I went in to the bathroom and found a pair of nylons I had washed earlier. I also put on a full-length slip that I had left in the bathroom, as experience taught me that men love slips for some reason.

As I fixed myself up, I started to realize that there was more to the problem than two lose holes. There was also the filthy talk. Bill trained me to instinctively shoot out vile remarks at the most erotic times, and it was reinforced by Al and his friends. It was re-awakened by Jack, Jamar, Bill again, Sam, and Pete. Mark had never heard me swear. What would I do if a statement came out uncontrollably?

I resolved that I had to somehow entice him to be the first with the sordid talk. I would then just be responding in lust to satisfy his desires! I thought about it, and he already started by saying he wanted to cum all over my face.

I was back to the bedroom and stood before Mark as he laid on the bed. I reached out for him and took his hand. I pulled him up to me. I held Mark close and whispered in his ear.

"Do you like what I've done for you?" I asked.

"Oh, God, yes," he murmured as he kissed me.

I then reversed the truth, whispering again as I licked his ear.

"We've been married so long, and I never knew you were so wild!"

His reply made me feel warm.

"You're just so incredibly beautiful," he said, "and I've always wanted to see cum on your face."

If he only knew how Bill felt the same way.

I smiled and kissed, him, telling him that his feelings were alright. I went on, telling him that wanted to please him, so he should never be afraid to tell me when he wants something.

Mark held me tight and whispered in my ear.

"You are so hot Andrea!"

I wanted to show him how hot I really was. I reached down to unbuckle his pants and pull them down. I was going to entice him to take me then and there.

I yanked down his pants and pulled out his stiffening cock. I dropped to my knees and worked the stiffening prick into my mouth. I rubbed the cock head on my lips as I looked up at him, gently scratching his balls with my fingernails.

It was time to start breaking in the filthy talk.

"So, you like having a banker work her fingers on your balls?" I asked.

He moaned.

"Do you like seeing your cock on my red lips?" I asked.

"God . . . yes," he moaned.

I jerked the cock as it started to grow. I don't think I had ever given my husband a hand job before.

"Do you like what I'm doing?" I asked.

"Oh yeah!" he said.

I jerked his cock slowly but firmly for a few minutes. I reach down and worked on his balls. I gently rubbed my nails over the sac again.

"How about this?" I asked.

"Oh fuck . . ." he moaned.

I went down on him again, going back and forth from licking his balls to sucking on his cock. In no time Mark was rock hard again, so I pulled off his pants to allow him to mount me more easily.

I laid down on the floor and lifted my slip. I spread my legs, my heels lifting them up. I rubbed my bush for him, pulling on my cunt lips every now and then. This was all something I hadn't done for Mark before, so he was pleasantly surprised when I did it.

I didn't want to spread my legs too wide, in case the truckers cum would start leaking out even though I douched. I had to get his cock in me fast to avoid the problem.

Reaching my arms out to him, I begged him.

"I think I know a lady banker who really needs to get laid."

He came down on the floor and kissed me, reaching down to feel my cunt. I was so terrified that he would feel Sam and Bill's cum in my slick cunt or, even worse, lick me and taste it!

Mark commented that I was wet, so I quickly responded that the whole scene was making me incredibly horny. I had to get him out from between my legs.

I reached for his cock and begged him.

"Fuck me . . . please fuck me now!"

Mark came in between my legs, guiding his cock to my hole. He slipped his cock right in, commenting that I really was wet.

I told Mark that the cum bath he gave me excited me beyond belief, and that I needed to get laid real bad. With that he reared back and started to stroke my cunt.

"Oh God, Mark," I yelled out.

"I loved the feel of your hot cum on my face," I moaned.

He grunted louder with my statement.

I had to get him talking the same way.

"God you're a stud . . . make your hot prick cream deep between your wife's legs," I said.

He pumped me harder, responding, "God, you're so fucking hot Andrea."

I didn't know if it was the scent of the cum on my face that was driving him mad with lust, or if it was the feel of the truckers' cum lubbing up his cock. But I wanted to add to it.

"Your cock feels so good, oh, Mark, give me your hard cock!"

He liked what was happening.

"You want my cock?" he asked.

"God yes," I moaned back.

"I want you to stroke that big cock off between my legs!"

Mark loved it! He stroked me long and deep, adding to the excitement.

"You want me to slam my prick in and shoot you full of cum?" he asked.

"Oh, fuck, splash my cunt with hot cum," I fired back.

"Stroke that cock off in me!!!"

It had been so long since Mark had a piece of ass, he was ready to blow his second load in no time. I could feel Mark's back tense up, so I reached behind and started stroking his ass.

"I need to feel your cum, Mark, please give me some hot cum."

His dick bolted deep inside me and started to shot.

I wrapped my legs tightly around him as he came, scratching his back. When Mark was done he fell on me.

I was worried that I went too far, but I tried to be gentle in easing him into it. He rolled over and hugged me, saying that he "really had a great fuck."

I was relieved that I made it through that, and more relieved that he apparently never noticed that my hole was wet and open from repeated fuckings. I couldn't believe that in hindsight I had worried for nothing. I felt bad that I put off this poor man needlessly, when he could have been satisfying my needs instead of that asshole Jack.

Mark and I laid in bed and started a conversation that had to last until two in the morning. We held each other and discussed love, sex, and fantasies. I sucked him off again as we talked about the more heated areas. Maybe we should have had this conversation earlier in our marriage, I don't know.

Mark has always been shy, and I was always tried to act like a reserved lady, until Bill got me that is. But Mark really was a stud in his own right, at least when we first met. I felt relieved by the end of the conversation, like a weight had been lifted from my shoulders.

Mark was in love with me as I was with him. He wanted so much for me to be happy. I truly believed that. We were a team, but we just had to start communicating about our sexuality and overcome a few obstacles.

I found out the Mark really loves filthy talk during sex, although he was always afraid to say too much because he didn't want to upset me. He also confessed that he's always wanted to fuck me in my work clothes.

The biggest remark that Mark made was on the topic of sex with other men. It took a little work to get it out of him. He started by telling me that he thought I was so beautiful and sexy that it turned him on to picture me having sex.

I asked him what he meant.

I eventually got him to confess that it wasn't just with him that he imagined, but with total strangers. The idea of another man taking me appealed to him, but it was so embarrassing he never told me.

I guess he was right. Before Bill and Al, I probably wouldn't have understood.

It really seemed that my problems were close to being solved. I thought I should try to nail things down, to test what we had discussed.

It was very late, but it was Friday night and the kids were at sleepovers. And Mark had already cum twice. He had never cum three times, with me at least. But this was too important to not take care of when the opportunity presented itself.

I told Mark to go downstairs, and that I would join him shortly.

After Mark left the bedroom, I put all of my make up on, carefully painted my lips with the brightest red lipstick I had, and sprayed on some perfume.

I then dressed up in one of my sexiest business suits to help make my husband's fantasy a reality. I put on black stockings; I knew he would go crazy over them. I put on my heels and went downstairs.

I thought Mark's eyes were going to pop out of his head when he saw me. He perked right up.

"Do you like?" I asked.

"You're so beautiful when you go to work," he responded.

I walked over to him and dropped to my knees.

Opening his robe, I took his soft cock in my hands.

"So, would you like it if I told you how much I love your cock?"

I popped it in my mouth and sucked hard. Pulling the cock out, I jacked it while it got hard. It took a while since Mark just got off, but I worked at it until it was stiff again.

"Oh God, you're such a fucking hot wife," he said, "I really missed this."

"Do you think I was I a prude, honey?" I asked.

"Well, sort of, but I figured with our work and the hassles it just didn't matter any more," he said.

"It does matter," I responded, "I want our marriage to last. So I'm going to do my part."

I sucked the cock in again as Mark started caressing my hair. Mark seemed to be relieved himself with my answer. Had he been feeling deprived? Perhaps he was.

Perhaps I was a sexual prude of a wife until Bill and Al seduced me.

By now Mark's cock was hard from the firm hand job I'd been giving him, so I lifted it back and started to lick his balls. I looked up at him with my tongue running across the sac.

"Do I look sexy licking a pair of big balls?"

He moaned his response.

I asked the next question.

"Am I sexy in my business suit? Do you think I could get laid?" I asked.

"Baby, you could laid by anyone you wanted," he responded.

"What would you do if some stranger had his cock stuck in my mouth?" I asked, immediately deep throating his cock as soon as the words were out of my mouth.

"I'd fuck your cunt," he said.

I moaned at his answer.

I slowly pulled the cock out to ask the next question.

"Where should we let this guy cum? Do you want him to dump it on your wife's face?"

I shot the cock back into my throat as his reply came groaning out.

"Oh, God, yes . . . Mmmmmm . . . and I'd flood your cunt too!"

I moaned again at the proposition, louder this time so he could clearly hear that it excited me.

I was making serious progress, so I stopped sucking to ask yet another question. Crawling up on his lap, I took his head in my arms and whispered in his ear.

"You want me to take his big cock up my cunt?" I asked.

"What if he made me moan like a whore, would you still love me?"

I wrapped his arms around me and we kissed. He stopped to give me his answer.

"Of course, I'd still love you, I don't ever want to lose you. It's not your fault you're a MILF!"

I don't think he realized what a formidable problem a ruined wife can present to a husband, but I knew I loved this man. We were certainly soul mates, so I took the next step with a firm resolution.

"Mark, if I sleep with other men to please you, I'm going to get pleased too. Are you sure you want to share my pussy with another cock?"

He told me he loved me, that he was a little queasy thinking about it, but that he really wanted to see another man take me.

What luck!

With that I straddled his cock and pushed myself down on it.

"Mark," I whispered in his ear as he was imbedded in my pussy, "this fucker is taking me."

We both moaned together.

"He's opening your wife's cunt. God, he's so big and he's going so deep!" I moaned.

Mark moaned back in approval.

"Oh fuck, his big cock feels so goo stroking my cunt!"

Mark moaned again, so I started stroking up and down on his cock harder. I felt an orgasm brewing in both of us.

"God, Mark, he gonna empty his balls in me," I moaned.

The intensity of our fucking picked up.

"Ohhhh . . . I feel his . . . cum, . . . its so . . . hot, its . . . sticking . . . to my . . . cunt."

That was it. We both exploded right there on the chair. It had to be the most intense act of sex Mark and I ever shared.

As we both came down from our lust high, I rested my head on him. I whispered in his ear.

"Mark, are we playing or are you serious," I asked as I laid in his arms.

"It's up to you sweetheart," he responded.

He paused for moment and thought.

"Andrea, I love you and I want you to be happy."

"What do you want?" I asked.

"Well, it would be great to see. Maybe just once."

"Well, let me think about it," I said, not wanting to appear to anxious.

I waited a minute as we both rested, thinking about what we were saying.

"I'll probably do it for you Mark,. . . " I said slowly, "because I love you . . . and we're going to make this marriage work."

"Yes, sweetheart," he responded, "I love you so much and we're going to make this work."

Finally! God finally helped me out of this wild predicament I had gotten myself into. Oh dear Lord, thank you so much!

I WAS FINALLY HAPPY! I FELT FULL, CONTENT, AND TRULY IN LOVE FOR THE FIRST TIME IN MY MARRIED LIFE!!!

Yes, my life was really about to change! With my wonderful husband!

My Story Continues

Ah, my new life!

Once I accepted that I would forever be a nymphomaniac, my life changed for the better. And now it would be truly fulfilled. I was going to become a happily married nymphomaniac.

The transformation of Mark was now started. It would soon be skillfully accomplished by my own mentor. Remember Al?

I invite you to read the rest of my story in *Husband's Tramp*!

Author's Perspective

Porn. Filth is what my mother always called it. The scourge of society is what some people call it. I call it healthy fun.

Now, to be clear, I'm talking about "mainstream" pornography. Once you cross the line into twisted acts or kiddie porn, all bets are off. The biggest problem I have with that kind of porn is that it hurts people. Children, for instance. They are too young to know what they are doing. It can destroy their bodies, their emotional well-being, and their lives. There's no room for tolerance when it comes to children.

It's all about choice, isn't it? A theme you will see in all of my books is choice. In each case, the woman had the choice of putting herself in the position to get laid. Nobody dragged them by the hair into a cave. The same is true for porn.

Face it. Some people NEVER get laid. My God, what would they do without porn? And what about unhappy couples? I'm sorry folks, but the sex life of couples does eventually die. It is a simple fact of life. The question is how you can resuscitate it. Or, better yet, keep it from ever getting ill in the first place. I suggest a healthy dose of porn.

You must all think I'm some kind of porn addict. Well, I do have a collection. My husband and I watch it regularly. And it's all locked up so our young children never get into it. That's safe. That's healthy.

And what about you? If you're reading this book, I have to presume that the topic interests you. Have you ever bought an adult DVD? If you haven't, let me suggest that they're not all that bad. (And no, I'm not an adult actress, so I'm not biassed one way or the other.)

Are you worried about the stigmatism? Well, I can understand that, because I am too. A lot of people are closet hypocrites. They go to church and lust over the hot mother sitting next to them. Or they surf porn on the Internet and jerk off at work. Remember, the industry is booming. How is that possible? *Because SOMEONE is buying it!* Perhaps you and I are more mainstream that we think.

It degrades women. Pa-lease. That is ridiculous. If it degrades women, it degrades men too. What, the women are show as being "forced" to do anal? Hmmm . . . watch a gay film and you might see a guy being forced too! I'm truly sorry, but I just don't see it.

I have heard all of the arguments for and against pornography. Frankly, and allow me to be blunt, I hear a lot of bullshit. Take, for instance, Shelly Lubben. I am sure that she passionately believes in her crusade against pornography. But is she being objective?

Shelley was a porn actress a long time ago. She says many women are drugged and forced to do porn. I am sorry, Shelley, but I absolutely do not believe that is true. In the 1970's when porn was just getting started, sure. I can see it having happened. I believe Linda Lovelace when she talks about what happened to her.

But now? I don't think so. 1000's of videos are created each year. Literally billions of dollars are spent by consumers for the products. Hell, if the sale of my books is any indication, the topic of sex is well received in America. My God, they even have a trade association, the AVN Media Network. And they give away awards, much like the Oscars. I don't see much of a need to do any forcing when that kind of machinery is in place.

From every documentary I've ever watched on the subject, it's clear that the studios have waiting lists of women who want to be porn stars. And why not? They are paid beyond belief for work they probably enjoy. And if they don't enjoy it? *Then why are they doing it?* Because they're broke? Because they're on drugs and need a fix? Hey, don't blame the industry for those women. They have no business being in adult videos; they are their because it's THEIR choice. They could always go to work for Burger King, but they decided not to.

I remember a documentary I saw with Nina Hartley and Kayden Kross. Now those beautiful ladies have their act together. They both argue passionately for pornography. And they should. The industry is good to them. Kudos, ladies.

That all having been said, I also have no doubt that some bad things do happen. I can see the small-time loser who wants to make a quick buck from a "porno" – but he (or she) has little resources. Get a girl, drug her up, and essentially rape her on video. Sure, I can see that happening. But guess what? THAT'S A CRIME. That's no different than rape on the streets. Just because you hate rape doesn't mean you should hate sex, right? Well, just because you (rightfully) hate those minority situations I described doesn't mean you should hate the entire adult industry.

So, use porn to spice up your sex life. Perhaps it's a way to bring your spouse around to a new way of thinking like Andrea did with Mark. However you decide, please . . . be happy, be safe!

– Jennifer